"Very few writers have the ran[ge] [...] [...]es zip, dip, twist and turn, move [...] [...]c. You are in for a treat. Enjoy!"

   – KAREN JOY FOWLER, aut[hor]

"Without Eileen Gunn, life as w[e] [...] [...] wouldn't recognize it. Among the five or six North Americans currently able to write short stories, she has not written anywhere near enough. But at least all of them are here in this book, an occasion for rejoicing from Manhattan to Makah."

   – URSULA K. LE GUIN, author of *Changing Planes*

"Gunn's stories are in another league entirely – like Sturgeon or Chiang, she's *sui generis* and anything but generic. Every one of these stories has a pleasing, sharp flavor unlike anything you've ever tasted. Especially the recipe for fruit crisp. Delicious."

   – CORY DOCTOROW, author of *Eastern Standard Tribe*
     and *Down and Out in the Magic Kingdom*, and
     co-editor of boingboing.net

"Reading this book is like getting to wear the eyeballs of a madwoman in your own sockets for a day. Nothing's going to look the same. Suddenly, the Richard Nixon Game Show and the girl with twenty-one fingers and the birds who need rest to die will make perfect sense. And your life will be better. So buy the damn book. It's brilliant."

   – WARREN ELLIS, author of the graphic novels
     Transmetropolitan and *Orbiter*

"Eileen Gunn's stories are like perfect little bullets, or maybe firecrackers. When you read Gunn, you remember that short fiction can be spare, beautiful, and deadly. I've been wanting to read this collection for a very long time."

   – KELLY LINK, author of *Stranger Things Happen*

"Eileen Gunn has a barbed-wire-sharp mind, an unsettling insight into the way the world works, and a wicked sense of humor, and her stories are just like her. From Cobain High to the Tower of Diminished Expectations, *Stable Strategies and Others* is a disconcerting, witty, delicious read!"

   – CONNIE WILLIS, author of *To Say Nothing of the Dog*

"Not caring to scavenge the slipstreamed Sargasso that typifies so much of today's American SF, Eileen Gunn gives us a lucid field guide to a veritable Galápagos of droll arcana and deeply-felt anomalies. Long-awaited, and worth the wait."

   – ROBERT MORALES, author of the graphic novel
   The Truth: Red, White, and Black

"'I awoke this morning to discover that bioengineering had made demands upon me during the night.' Who hasn't had mornings like that? It's a strange life we live, and it gets stranger every day: Eileen Gunn knows as much. A sharp-eyed student of mantises, windswept deserts, Fibonacci numbers, and Richard Nixon, she unblinkingly faces this brave new world as if she'd started off the day sharing coffee with Kafka, trading knowing remarks about the preternatural weirdness of the world. Gunn shows us vistas and scenarios possible and improbable, suggests events that may or may not have happened, and invites us to stretch our minds and imaginations as she does her own. This book contains no end of treasures and pleasures for anyone fortunate enough to come to it, and I'm glad to have it close at hand."

   – GREGORY MCNAMEE, author of *Blue Mountains Far Away*
   and *Christ on the Mount of Olives and Other Stories*

"...perfectly realized horror..."
   – STEPHEN KING, about "Spring Conditions"

STABLE STRATEGIES AND OTHERS

EILEEN GUNN

Stable Strategies
AND OTHERS

TACHYON PUBLICATIONS
SAN FRANCISCO, CALIFORNIA

Book design & composition by John D. Berry. The typeface is Dolly.

Tachyon Publications
1459 18th Street, #139
San Francisco CA 94107
(415) 285-5615
www.tachyonpublications.com

Distributed to the trade by Independent Publishers Group.

Edited by Jacob Weisman

ISBN: 1-892391-18-X

Printed in the United States of America
by Phoenix Color Corporation

First edition: 2004

0 9 8 7 6 5 4 3 2 1

CONTENTS

To my partner John D. Berry
and my nieces Erin Gunn and Kelsey Gunn

ACKNOWLEDGMENTS

MY THANKS TO Paul G. Allen, Leota Anthony, Brian Attebery, Steve Ballmer, Stephen P. Brown, A. Fluffy Bunny, Jonathan Canick, Susan Casper, Victoria Cooper, Karen Corsano, Ann M. Dailey, Ellen Datlow, Avram Davidson, Cory Doctorow, Gardner Dozois, Ron Drummond, L. Timmel Duchamp, Warren Ellis, Carol Emshwiller, Karen Fishler, Karen Joy Fowler, Jeffrey Frederick, The Fugs, Bill Gates, William Gibson, Jeanne Gomoll, Joe and Gay Haldeman, Dottie Hall, Sam Hamill, Rowland Hanson, Rachel Holmen, the Holy Modal Rounders, Leslie Howle, Nicholas D. Humez, Michael Hurley, James Patrick Kelly, John Kessel, Ellen Klages, Damon Knight, Mari Kotani, Eleanor Lang, Ursula K. Le Guin, Kelly Link, Diane Mapes, Don McAlister, Vonda N. McIntyre, Bob Morales, Pat Murphy, Debbie Notkin, Paul Novitski, Robert O'Brien, Spike Parsons, Linn Prentis, John S. Quarterman, Joanna Russ, Geoff Ryman, Jessica Amanda Salmonson, Tony Sarowitz, Peter H. Salus, Kate Schaefer, Scott Scidmore, Nisi Shawl, Willie Siros, Bruce Sterling, Michael Swanwick, Avon Swofford, Takayuki Tatsumi, Tamara Vining, Howard Waldrop, Don Webb, Wendy Wees, Jacob Weisman, Henry Wessells, Leslie What, Kate Wilhelm, Sheila Williams, Connie Willis, Robin Scott Wilson, Jack Womack, and to my family, and to all the others who have helped make my writing better and have kept me creatively and financially on track.

She's the Business

William Gibson

WHEN I WAS A BOY of thirteen or so, living in a small Virginia town and thinking of almost nothing but the science fiction I read, I learned that the genre was thought of as comprising a "ghetto." Not by anyone in my immediate vicinity, but by the inhabitants of that supposed ghetto: the writers, editors, and (to some extent) readers of the stuff. Most people in my immediate vicinity, had they been asked, would have been unlikely to have described science fiction as a ghetto; "trash," maybe, "balderdash," but hardly a ghetto.

A couple of years later, I myself would have been reluctant to describe science fiction as a ghetto – mainly because I so badly wanted it to be not a ghetto but a bohemia. I had never seen a bohemia, but somehow I knew I wanted one. I had never seen a ghetto either, unless you counted the houses of the local blacks, which tended to be smaller and more dilapidated than the houses of whites, and to be clustered together somewhat at a distance.

I wanted a bohemia so much that I shortly left that town, and science fiction as well, in search of one. And found it (which proved easier than I had expected, given my timing).

Quite a long time later, nearly a decade, when for various peculiar reasons I found myself returning to science fiction, first as a reader and then as tyro writer, it still didn't look much like a ghetto to me. Or, alas, much like a bohemia.

What it most resembled, it seemed to me, was a small town. A damned peculiar one, when you started looking around, but nonetheless subject to most of the complaints typical of sub-urban burgs: parochialism, provinciality, the literary equivalent of xenophobia. A worldview best characterized by this weird dysmorphia: that everything that wasn't "the genre" (i.e. the whole of world literature other than science fiction) was "the mainstream." This mainstream seemed generally to be regarded either as simply another (and generally inferior) genre, or the enemy, or (generally) both.

To add to the general weirdness, SFville was (and remains) a distributed entity, non-geographical.

For instance, though Old Glory flew from virtually every clap-board façade on Main Street, there was a British Quarter (one that many townspeople prided themselves on not yet having managed to visit). All of this had sprung up, long before the advent of email, via a marvelous construction some now refer to as the Paper Internet, and indeed there was not yet email when I first met Eileen Gunn.

Which was right at the very beginning of what would become my career, and what a very good and indeed utterly crucial person she was to meet. For starts, she wasn't insane. For some reason, my earliest cohort in SFville numbered more than a few who were mad as sacks of rats. Eileen was a steadying influence, though never even remotely a dull one.

I have no idea when she'd arrived there, or how. I only know that when I stepped down from the bus, as it were, she was there to greet me and show me around, and was so evidently an urbane and delightfully witty person, so clearly not of that dysmorphic literary mindset, and yet she knew the place. Knew it in fractal detail, in every oddity of its culture, and seemed to appreciate it that way as well, exactly as she might some yurt-circle in Central Asia. While I, in my seething insecurity as desperate not-yet-writer, would periodically hiss at her, from between tensely raised shoulders, about hicks and one-horseness. At which, being that rarest of critters, the nerd with gloriously ample social skills, she would introduce me to yet another interesting resident (though these might range from the undeniably great Avram Davidson to the still-unsung creator of a species of slash fiction devoted exclusively to the passions of shaved Wookiees).

And she was a writer. Not merely a career-tourist but one with the sign blazoned full across her forehead, a lifer. She also, as Howard Waldrop tells us in his afterword, proved to be an even slower writer than Howard Waldrop. She became a sort of saint to me for this, as I was capable from the start of spending an entire twelve-hour stretch before the (then) typewriter, debating verb-tense choices in some minor clause. And not being able, finally, to decide. In addition, I suffer from a torch-bearing mob of inner voices, constantly shouting that whatever I've just written is as attractive as hairball macramé. Eileen had her own inner mob as well; excessive quality control issues, you might say.

The contents of this collection, having somehow conspired to make it past the iron-shod galoshes of Gunnian quality control, comprise the short-fiction oeuvre, so far, of someone whose thoroughly hands-on grasp of science fiction, and whose vision of what it *could* be, change things. The genre today is still a small town, albeit somewhat gentrified on the outskirts, with its core population numbering, I'd guess, not many more than a thousand. Among that thousand or so, Eileen Gunn's innate sensibilities and cultural smarts have designated her a nodal entity, one of those human intersections where people and ideas meet, and out of which things change.

The exterior manifestations of this would be her careers as editor, teacher and Clarion West honcho, but the real mojo is working at some deeper level altogether. She is, quite simply, "the business."

I enjoyed each of the pieces collected herein, but my favorites are "Fellow Americans," a brilliant recursive fable in which Richard Nixon finds the career and the serenity that eluded him in our world, the sadly hilarious "Nirvana High" (with Leslie What) and "Green Fire," which has four authors, a situation akin to having four heads and being a very good dancer.

All ample proof that Eileen Gunn really is the business. ⟡

Vancouver, 5 14 04

The Secret of Writing

Eileen Gunn

OCTOBER, 1987. Armadillocon, then the hippest science fiction convention on the face of the earth. I ran into Bill Gibson.

"We have to talk," he said. "I've discovered the secret of writing."

Gibson is a master of the conversational hook.

We sat down. We got caught up. Someone came and dragged Bill off to opening ceremonies, of which he was an essential part. Then things moved faster and faster, and pretty soon the weekend was over.

Two weeks later, at home in Seattle, I answered the phone. It was Gibson. "I forgot to tell you the secret of writing," he said.

"Okay," I said. "What's the secret of writing?"

A beat, for emphasis. Then: "You must learn to overcome your very natural and appropriate revulsion for your own work."

It was the most useful writing advice anyone has ever given me. ⟐

Hooray for Eileen!

Michael Swanwick

Hooray for Eileen and her bully machine
That turns out such volumes of stuff!
Some think it queer
She's so seldom here
Few find her absence enough.

She lives in this town
(At least, here's where's she's foun
d); She is graced with a runcible style.
Some think that she should
Write what *they* wish they could
But she freezes them out with a smile.

Let's all celebrate
Before it's too late
And time's wingéd chariot's seen,
That queen of the text,
Seldom sour, never vexed,
Eileen! — and her bully machine. ⸙

Michael Swanwick
July 16, 1994
Seattle

STABLE STRATEGIES AND OTHERS

Stable Strategies for Middle Management

Our cousin the insect has an external skeleton made of shiny brown chitin, a material that is particularly responsive to the demands of evolution. Just as bioengineering has sculpted our bodies into new forms, so evolution has changed the early insect's chewing mouthparts into her descendants' chisels, siphons, and stilettos, and has molded from the chitin special tools — pockets to carry pollen, combs to clean her compound eyes, notches on which she can fiddle a song.

— From the popular science program *Insect People!*

I AWOKE THIS MORNING TO DISCOVER that bioengineering had made demands upon me during the night. My tongue had turned into a stiletto, and my left hand now contained a small chitinous comb, as if for cleaning a compound eye. Since I didn't have compound eyes, I thought that perhaps this presaged some change to come.

I dragged myself out of bed, wondering how I was going to drink my coffee through a stiletto. Was I now expected to kill my breakfast, and dispense with coffee entirely? I hoped I was not evolving into a creature whose survival depended on early-morning alertness. My circadian rhythms would no doubt keep pace with any physical changes, but my unevolved soul was repulsed at the thought of my waking cheerfully at dawn, ravenous for some wriggly little creature that had arisen even earlier.

I looked down at Greg, still asleep, the edge of our red and white quilt pulled up under his chin. His mouth had changed during the night too, and seemed to contain some sort of a long probe. Were we growing apart?

I reached down with my unchanged hand and touched his hair. It was still shiny brown, soft and thick, luxurious. But along his cheek, under his beard, I could feel patches of sclerotin, as the flexible chitin in his skin was slowly hardening to an impermeable armor.

He opened his eyes, staring blearily forward without moving his head. I could see him move his mouth cautiously, examining its internal changes. He turned his head and looked up at me, rubbing his hair slightly into my hand.

"Time to get up?" he asked. I nodded. "Oh God," he said. He said this every morning. It was like a prayer.

"I'll make coffee," I said. "Do you want some?"

He shook his head slowly. "Just a glass of apricot nectar," he said. He unrolled his long, rough tongue and looked at it, slightly cross-eyed. "This is real interesting, but it wasn't in the catalog. I'll be sipping lunch from flowers pretty soon. That ought to draw a second glance at Duke's."

"I thought account execs were *expected* to sip their lunches," I said.

"Not from the flower arrangements…," he said, still exploring the odd shape of his mouth. Then he looked up at me and reached up from under the covers. "Come here."

It had been a while, I thought. And I had to get to work. But he did smell terribly attractive. Perhaps he was developing aphrodisiac scent glands. I climbed back under the covers and stretched my body against his. We were both developing chitinous knobs and odd lumps that made this less than comfortable. "How am I supposed to kiss you with a stiletto in my mouth?" I asked.

"There are other things to do. New equipment presents new possibilities." He pushed the covers back and ran his unchanged hands down my body from shoulder to thigh. "Let me know if my tongue is too rough."

It was not.

Fuzzy-minded, I got out of bed for the second time and drifted into the kitchen.

Measuring the coffee into the grinder, I realized that I was no longer interested in drinking it, although it was diverting for a moment to spear the beans with my stiletto. What was the damn thing for, anyhow? I wasn't sure I wanted to find out.

Putting the grinder aside, I poured a can of apricot nectar into a tulip glass. Shallow glasses were going to be a problem for Greg in the future, I thought. Not to mention solid food.

My particular problem, however, if I could figure out what I was supposed to eat for breakfast, was getting to the office in time for my 10 A.M. meeting. Maybe I'd just skip breakfast. I dressed quickly and dashed out the door before Greg was even out of bed.

Thirty minutes later, I was more or less awake and sitting in the small conference room with the new marketing manager, listening to him lay out his plan for the Model 2000 launch.

In signing up for his bioengineering program, Harry had chosen specialized primate adaptation, B-E Option No. 4. He had evolved into a text-book example: small and long-limbed, with forward-facing eyes for judging distances and long, grasping fingers to keep him from falling out of his tree.

He was dressed for success in a pin-striped three-piece suit that fit his simian proportions perfectly. I wondered what premium he paid for custom-made. Or did he patronize a ready-to-wear shop that catered especially to primates?

I listened as he leaped agilely from one ridiculous marketing premise to the next. Trying to borrow credibility from mathematics and engineering, he used wildly metaphoric bizspeak, "factoring in the need for pipeline throughput," "fine-tuning the media mix," without even cracking a smile.

Harry had been with the company only a few months, straight out of business school. He saw himself as a much-needed infusion of talent. I didn't like him, but I envied him his ability to root through his subconscious and toss out one half-formed idea after another. I know he felt it reflected badly on me that I didn't join in and spew forth a random selection of promotional suggestions.

I didn't think much of his marketing plan. The advertising section was a textbook application of theory with no practical basis. I had two options: I could force him to accept a solution that would work, or I could yes him to death, making sure everybody understood it was his idea. I knew which path I'd take.

"Yeah, we can do that for you," I told him. "No problem." We'd see which of us would survive and which was hurtling to an evolutionary dead end.

Although Harry had won his point, he continued to belabor it. My attention wandered — I'd heard it all before. His voice was the hum of an air conditioner, a familiar, easily ignored background noise. I drowsed and new emotions stirred in me, yearnings to float through moist air currents, to land on bright surfaces, to engorge myself with warm, wet food.

Adrift in insect dreams, I became sharply aware of the bare skin of Harry's arm, between his gold-plated watchband and his rolled-up sleeve, as he manipulated papers on the conference room table. He smelled delicious, like a pepperoni pizza or a charcoal-broiled hamburger. I realized he probably wouldn't taste as good as he smelled. But I was hungry. My stiletto-like tongue was there for a purpose, and it wasn't to skewer cubes of tofu. I leaned over his arm and braced myself against the back of his hand, probing with my stylets to find a capillary.

Harry noticed what I was doing and swatted me sharply on the side of the head. I pulled away before he could hit me again.

"We were discussing the Model 2000 launch. Or have you forgotten?" he said, rubbing his arm.

"Sorry. I skipped breakfast this morning." I was embarrassed.

"Well, get your hormones adjusted, for chrissake." He was annoyed, and I couldn't really blame him. "Let's get back to the media allocation issue, if you can keep your mind on it. I've got another meeting at eleven in Building Two."

Inappropriate feeding behavior was not unusual in the company, and corporate etiquette sometimes allowed minor lapses to pass without pursuit. Of course, I could no longer hope that he would support me on moving some money out of the direct-mail budget....

During the remainder of the meeting, my glance kept drifting through the open door of the conference room, toward a large decorative plant in the hall, one of those oases of generic greenery that dot the corporate landscape. It didn't look succulent exactly — it obviously wasn't what I would have preferred to eat if I hadn't been so hungry — but I wondered if I swung both ways?

I grabbed a handful of the broad leaves as I left the room and carried them back to my office. With my tongue, I probed a vein in the thickest part of a leaf. It wasn't so bad. Tasted green. I sucked them dry and tossed the husks in the wastebasket.

I was still omnivorous, at least — female mosquitoes don't eat plants. So the process wasn't complete....

I got a cup of coffee, for company, from the kitchenette and sat in my office with the door closed and wondered what was happening to me. The incident with Harry disturbed me. Was I turning into a mosquito? If so, what the hell kind of good was that supposed to do me? The company didn't have any use for a whining loner, a bloodsucker.

There was a knock at the door, and my boss stuck his head in. I nodded and gestured him into my office. He sat down in the visitor's chair on the other side of my desk. From the look on his face, I could tell Harry had talked to him already.

Tom Samson was an older guy, pre-bioengineering. He was well versed in stimulus-response techniques, but had somehow never made it to the top job. I liked him, but then that was what he intended. Without sacrificing authority, he had pitched his appearance, his gestures, the tone of his voice, to the warm end of the spectrum. Even though I knew what he was doing, it worked.

He looked at me with what appeared to be sympathy, but was actually a practiced sign stimulus, intended to defuse any fight-or-flight response. "Is there something bothering you, Margaret?"

"Bothering me? I'm hungry, that's all. I get short-tempered when I'm hungry."

Watch it, I thought. He hasn't referred to the incident; leave it for him to bring up. I made my mind go bland and forced myself to see his eyes. A shifty gaze is a guilty gaze.

Tom just looked at me, biding his time, waiting for me to put myself on the spot. My coffee smelt burnt, but I stuck my tongue in it and pretended to drink. "I'm just not human until I've had my coffee in the morning." Sounded phoney. Shut up, I thought.

This was the opening that Tom was waiting for. "That's what I wanted to talk to you about, Margaret." He sat there, hunched over in a relaxed way, like a mountain gorilla, unthreatened by natural enemies. "I just talked to Harry Winthrop, and he said you were trying to suck his blood during a meeting on marketing strategy." He paused for a moment to check my reaction, but the neutral expression was fixed on my face and I said nothing. His face changed to project disappointment. "You know, when we noticed you were developing three distinct body segments, we had great hopes for you. But your actions just don't reflect the social and organizational development we expected."

He paused, and it was my turn to say something in my defense. "Most insects are solitary, you know. Perhaps the company erred in hoping for a termite or an ant. I'm not responsible for that."

"Now, Margaret," he said, his voice simulating genial reprimand. "This isn't the jungle, you know. When you signed those consent forms, you agreed to let the B-E staff mold you into a more useful corporate organism. But this isn't nature, this is man reshaping nature. It doesn't follow the old rules. You can truly be anything you want to be. But you have to cooperate."

"I'm doing the best I can," I said, cooperatively. "I'm putting in eighty hours a week."

"Margaret, the quality of your work is not an issue. It's your interactions with others that you have to work on. You have to learn to work as part of the group. I just cannot permit such backbiting to continue. I'll have Arthur get you an appointment this afternoon with the B-E counselor." Arthur was his secretary. He knew everything that happened in the department and mostly kept his mouth shut.

"I'd be a social insect if I could manage it," I muttered as Tom left my office. "But I've never known what to say to people in bars."

For lunch I met Greg and our friend David Detlor at a health-food restaurant that advertises fifty different kinds of fruit nectar. We'd never eaten there before, but Greg knew he'd love the place. It was already a favorite of David's, and he still has all his teeth, so I figured it would be OK with me.

David was there when I arrived, but not Greg. David works for the company too, in a different department. He, however, has proved remarkably resistant to corporate blandishment. Not only has he never undertaken B-E, he hasn't even bought a three-piece suit. Today he was wearing chewed-up blue jeans and a flashy Hawaiian shirt, of a type that was cool about ten years ago.

"Your boss lets you dress like that?" I asked.

"We have this agreement. I don't tell her she has to give me a job, and she doesn't tell me what to wear."

David's perspective on life is very different from mine. I don't think it's just that he's in R&D and I'm in Advertising — it's more basic than that. Where he sees the world as a bunch of really neat but optional puzzles put there for his enjoyment, I see it as…well, as a series of SATs.

"So what's new with you guys?" he asked, while we stood around waiting for a table.

"Greg's turning into a goddamn butterfly. He went out last week and bought a dozen Italian silk sweaters. It's not a corporate look."

"He's not a corporate *guy*, Margaret."

"Then why is he having all this B-E done if he's not even going to use it?"

"He's dressing up a little. He just wants to look nice. Like Michael Jackson, you know?"

I couldn't tell whether David was kidding me or not. Then he started telling me about his music, this barbershop quartet that he sings in. They were going to dress in black leather for the next competition and sing Shel Silverstein's "Come to Me, My Masochistic Baby."

"It'll knock them on their tails," he said gleefully. "We've already got a great arrangement."

"Do you think it will win, David?" It seemed too weird to please the judges in that sort of a show.

"Who cares?" said David. He didn't look worried.

Just then Greg showed up. He was wearing a cobalt blue silk sweater with a copper green design on it. Italian. He was also wearing a pair of dangly earrings shaped like bright blue airplanes. We were shown to a table near a display of carved vegetables.

"This is great," said David. "Everybody wants to sit near the vegetables. It's where you sit to be *seen* in this place." He nodded to Greg. "I think it's your sweater."

"It's the butterfly in my personality," said Greg. "Waiters never used to do stuff like this for me. I always got the table next to the espresso machine."

If Greg was going to go on about the perks that come with being a butterfly, I was going to change the subject.

"David, how come you still haven't signed up for B-E?" I asked. "The company pays half the cost, and they don't ask questions."

David screwed up his mouth, raised his hands to his face, and made small, twitching, insect gestures, as if grooming his nose and eyes. "I'm doing OK the way I am."

Greg chuckled at this, but I was serious. "You'll get ahead faster with a little adjustment. Plus you're showing a good attitude, you know, if you do it."

"I'm getting ahead faster than I want to right now — it looks like I won't be able to take the three months off that I wanted this summer."

"Three months?" I was astonished. "Aren't you afraid you won't have a job to come back to?"

"I could live with that," said David calmly, opening his menu.

The waiter took our orders. We sat for a moment in a companionable silence, the self-congratulation that follows ordering high-fiber foodstuffs. Then I told them the story of my encounter with Harry Winthrop.

"There's something wrong with me," I said. "Why suck his blood? What good is that supposed to do me?"

"Well," said David, "*you* chose this schedule of treatments. Where did you want it to go?"

"According to the catalog," I said, "the No.2 Insect Option is supposed to make me into a successful competitor for a middle-management niche, with triggerable responses that can be useful in gaining entry to upper hierarchical levels. Unquote." Of course, that was just ad talk — I didn't really expect it to do all that. "That's what I want. I want to be in charge. I want to be the boss."

"Maybe you should go back to BioEngineering and try again," said Greg. "Sometimes the hormones don't do what you expect. Look at my tongue, for instance." He unfurled it gently and rolled it back into his mouth. "Though I'm sort of getting to like it." He sucked at his drink, making disgusting slurping sounds. He didn't need a straw.

"Don't bother with it, Margaret," said David firmly, taking a cup of rosehip tea from the waiter. "Bioengineering is a waste of time and money and millions of years of evolution. If human beings were intended to be managers, we'd have evolved pin-striped body covering."

"That's cleverly put," I said, "but it's dead wrong."

The waiter brought our lunches, and we stopped talking as he put them in front of us. It seemed like the anticipatory silence of three very hungry people, but was in fact the polite silence of three people who have been brought up not to argue in front of disinterested bystanders. As soon as he left, we resumed the discussion.

"I mean it," David said. "The dubious survival benefits of management aside, bioengineering is a waste of effort. Harry Winthrop, for instance, doesn't really need B-E at all. Here he is, fresh out of business school, audibly buzzing with lust for a high-level management position. Basically he's just marking time until a presidency opens up somewhere. And what gives him the edge over you is his youth and inexperience, not some specialized primate adaptation."

"Well," I said with some asperity, "he's not constrained by a knowledge of what's failed in the past, that's for sure. But saying that doesn't solve my problem, David. Harry's signed up. I've signed up. The changes are under way and I don't have any choice."

I squeezed a huge glob of honey into my tea from a plastic bottle shaped like a teddy bear. I took a sip of the tea; it was minty and very sweet. "And now I'm turning into the wrong kind of insect. It's ruined my ability to deal with Product Marketing."

"Oh, give it a rest!" said Greg suddenly. "This is *so* boring. I don't want to hear any more talk about corporate hugger-mugger. Let's talk about something that's fun."

I had had enough of Greg's lepidopterate lack of concentration. "Something that's *fun?* I've invested all my time and most of my genetic material in this job. This is all the goddamn fun there is."

The honeyed tea made me feel hot. My stomach itched — I wondered if I was having an allergic reaction. I scratched, and not discreetly. My hand came out from under my shirt full of little waxy scales. What the hell was going on under there? I tasted one of the scales; it was wax all right. Worker bee changes? I couldn't help myself — I stuffed the wax into my mouth.

David was busying himself with his alfalfa sprouts, but Greg looked disgusted. "That's gross, Margaret." He made a face, sticking his tongue part way out. Talk about gross. "Can't you wait until after lunch?"

I was doing what came naturally, and did not dignify his statement with a response. There was a side dish of bee pollen on the table. I took a spoonful and mixed it with the wax, chewing noisily. I'd had a rough morning, and bickering with Greg wasn't making the day more pleasant.

Besides, neither he nor David had any respect for my position in the company. Greg doesn't take my job seriously at all. And David simply does what he wants to do, regardless of whether it makes any money, for himself or anyone else. He was giving me a back-to-nature lecture, and it was far too late for that.

This whole lunch was a waste of time. I was tired of listening to them, and felt an intense urge to get back to work. A couple of quick stings distracted them both: I had the advantage of surprise. I ate some more honey and quickly waxed them over. They were soon hibernating side by side in two large octagonal cells.

I looked around the restaurant. People were rather nervously pretending not to have noticed. I called the waiter over and handed him my credit card. He signaled to several bus boys, who brought a covered cart and took Greg and David away. "They'll eat themselves out of that by Thursday afternoon," I told him. "Store them on their sides in a warm, dry place, away from direct heat." I left a large tip.

I walked back to the office, feeling a bit ashamed of myself. A couple days of hibernation weren't going to make Greg or David more sympathetic to my problems. And they'd be real mad when they got out.

I didn't used to do things like that. I used to be more patient, didn't I? More appreciative of the diverse spectrum of human possibility. More interested in sex and television.

This job was not doing much for me as a warm, personable human being. At the very least, it was turning me into an unpleasant lunch companion. Whatever had made me think I wanted to get into management anyway?

The money, maybe.

But that wasn't all. It was the challenge, the chance to do something new, to control the total effort instead of just doing part of a project....

The money too, though. There were other ways to get money. Maybe I should just kick the supports out from under the damned job and start over again.

I saw myself sauntering into Tom's office, twirling his visitor's chair around and falling into it. The words "I quit" would force their way out, almost against my will. His face would show surprise — feigned, of course. By then I'd have to go through with it. Maybe I'd put my feet up on his desk. And then —

But was it possible to just quit, to go back to being the person I used to be? No, I wouldn't be able to do it. I'd never be a management virgin again.

I walked up to the employee entrance at the rear of the building. A suction device next to the door sniffed at me, recognized my scent, and clicked the door open. Inside, a group of new employees, trainees, were clustered near the door, while a personnel officer introduced them to the lock and let it familiarize itself with their pheromones.

On the way down the hall, I passed Tom's office. The door was open. He was at his desk, bowed over some papers, and looked up as I went by.

"Ah, Margaret," he said. "Just the person I want to talk to. Come in for a minute, would you." He moved a large file folder onto the papers in front of him on his desk, and folded his hands on top of them. "So glad you were passing by." He nodded toward a large, comfortable chair. "Sit down.

"We're going to be doing a bit of restructuring in the department," he began, "and I'll need your input, so I want to fill you in now on what will be happening."

I was immediately suspicious. Whenever Tom said, "I'll need your input," he meant everything was decided already.

"We'll be reorganizing the whole division, of course," he continued, drawing little boxes on a blank piece of paper. He'd mentioned this at the department meeting last week.

"Now, your area subdivides functionally into two separate areas, wouldn't you say?"

"Well —"

"Yes," he said thoughtfully, nodding his head as though in agreement. "That would be the way to do it." He added a few lines and a few more boxes. From what I could see, it meant that Harry would do all the interesting stuff, and I'd sweep up afterwards.

"Looks to me as if you've cut the balls out of my area and put them over into Harry Winthrop's," I said.

"Ah, but your area is still very important, my dear. That's why I don't have you actually reporting to Harry." He gave me a smile like a lie.

He had put me in a tidy little bind. After all, he was my boss. If he was going to take most of my area away from me, as it seemed he was, there wasn't much I could do to stop him. And I would be better off if we both pretended that I hadn't experienced any loss of status. That way I kept my title and my salary.

"Oh, I see," I said. "Right."

It dawned on me that this whole thing had been decided already, and that Harry Winthrop probably knew all about it. He'd probably even wangled a raise out of it. Tom had called me in here to make it look casual, to make it look as though I had something to say about it. I'd been set up.

This made me mad. There was no question of quitting now. I'd stick around and fight. My eyes blurred, unfocused, refocused again. Compound eyes! The promise of the small comb in my hand was fulfilled! I felt a deep chemical understanding of the ecological system I was now a part of. I knew where I fit in. And I knew what I was going to do. It was inevitable now, hard-wired in at the DNA level.

The strength of this conviction triggered another change in the chitin, and for the first time I could actually feel the rearrangement of my mouth and nose, a numb tickling like inhaling seltzer water. The stiletto receded and mandibles jutted forth, rather like Katherine Hepburn. Form and function achieved an orgasmic synchronicity. As my jaw pushed forward, mantis-like, it also opened, and I pounced on Tom and bit his head off.

He leaped from his desk and danced headless about the office.

I felt in complete control of myself as I watched him and continued the conversation. "About the Model 2000 launch," I said. "If we factor in the demand for pipeline throughput and adjust the media mix just a bit, I think we can present a very tasty little package to Product Marketing by the end of the week."

Tom continued to strut spasmodically, making vulgar copulative motions. Was I responsible for evoking these mantid reactions? I was unaware of a sexual component in our relationship.

I got up from the visitor's chair and sat behind his desk, thinking about what had just happened. It goes without saying that I was surprised at my own actions. I mean, irritable is one thing, but biting people's heads off is quite another. But I have to admit that my second thought was, well, this certainly is a useful strategy, and should make a considerable difference in my ability to advance myself. Hell of a lot more productive than sucking people's blood.

Maybe there was something after all to Tom's talk about having the proper attitude.

And, of course, thinking of Tom, my third reaction was

regret. He really had been a likeable guy, for the most part. But what's done is done, you know, and there's no use chewing on it after the fact.

I buzzed his assistant on the intercom. "Arthur," I said, "Mr. Samson and I have come to an evolutionary parting of the ways. Please have him re-engineered. And charge it to Personnel."

Now I feel an odd itching on my forearms and thighs. Notches on which I might fiddle a song? ◊

I wrote this story after I left Microsoft, way back in the Pleistocene. It was nominated for the Hugo award in 1989. It's one of my few stories with an unreservedly happy ending, for which I am indebted to my fierce friend Jessica Amanda Salmonson.

The story is generally regarded as a pastiche on "Metamorphosis," but, if I recall correctly, that isn't what I had in mind when I started it. I felt that working at Microsoft had irrevocably changed my personality, and I was trying to describe the evolution I had undergone. I was having a problem with the ending, so I described the story to Jessica one evening, when we were sitting around in my living room.

"I bet Kafka did it better," she snapped.

Omigod, I thought. Kafka *did* do it better. What a fool I was. I was instantly plunged into depression. Kafka had done it better, for sure.

"Well, let me see it," she said. I went and got it from my office, and she read it right there.

"Hmmph," she snorted, on finishing it. "That's *nothing* like Kafka."

That cheered me up immediately. No matter that it had problems with the ending: at least it was nothing like Kafka.

Jessica didn't like the ending, which was different from the one you just read. "How come she doesn't just bite the guy's head off?" she asked.

I dismissed the idea immediately. That would never have worked at Microsoft. It would have been a dead-end strategy for sure.

And then I came to my senses: I wasn't *at* Microsoft any more. I was writing a short story.

That was the beginning of my recovery.

Fellow Americans

"...AND NOW, the man you *loved to hate*, the man you loved *too late*, the man *every*one loves to second-guess, America's own *Tricky Dick!*"

Applause, and the strains of "Let Me Call You Sweetheart." A tanned, well-groomed man in a blue blazer and grey slacks walks between the curtains.

He raises his hands above his head in the familiar double V-for-Victory salute to acknowledge the applause, then gestures for quiet.

"Thanks for the hand, folks." His voice is deep, quiet, and sincere. "You know, I needed that applause today." A catch in his throat. "Right before the show, I was on my way down here to the studio..." He shakes his head slightly, as if contemplating the role that Chance plays in Life. "An elderly lady came up to me, and she introduced herself, and then she said, 'Oh, Dick, I'm so pleased to meet you, you know you were my all-time *favorite* presidential candidate...'" He lets the compliment hang there a second, as if savoring it. "...after Jack Kennedy, of course."

The audience laughs, appreciating the host who can tell a joke at his own expense. When the laughter has diminished, but before it stops completely, he continues.

"Speaking of politics, why is everybody picking on Dan Quayle these days?" He looks from face to face in the audience, as if for an answer. "He hasn't done anything." An artful pause. "And, as I know from my own turn at the job, he probably won't get to do anything in the future, either." More laughter, stronger.

He holds up a hand to stop them. "Seriously, folks, just the other day I was sharing a story with Dan — a story about two brothers." His voice is soft, as if confessing a family secret. "One ran away to sea and the other grew up to be vice-president...." He hunches his shoulders and looks down at the floor, shaking his head pensively. "Neither one of them was ever heard from again," he adds lugubriously. The audience howls with laughter and applauds enthusiastically.

The Governor of New York City looked out the small round window at the top of the ten-story Tower of Diminished Expectations and, through dirty glass, surveyed the 1990 New York World's Fair. He and Ethel had walked the 280 stairs to the top, and they were more than slightly out of breath.

Their hostess, a lovely young woman in a miniskirted uniform and a startlingly authentic retro-Sixties bubble haircut, pointed out the three festival areas they had just toured — the glass and steel pavilions of the Private Sector, the workaday plastic stucco of the Public Sector, and the tattered, colorful tents of the makeshift Alternative Fair.

The Private Sector, a promotional crankshaft for the wheels of industry, included the Minamata Pavilion, an entire building made from the byproducts of engineered bacteria raised on toxic waste; MacRainforest, a model cattle ranch from the Amazon; and Weyerhaeuser's Walking Woods, a moving strip of biotope that rolled past onlookers as robot animals sang about the delightful variety of life in a clear-cut woodland.

In contrast, the Public Sector presented a cluster of low-budget homilies on the virtues of self-sufficiency and making-do-with-less — preparing people to live in a world of survivable nukes, reduced government services, lowered wages and raised taxes. Its highlights were a low-level nuclear waste dump, which was built right on the site and would be entombed there after the Fair closed, and a mammoth exhibit on Local Empowerment, made entirely by gradeschool children out of papier-mâché.

The Alternative Fair was an amorphous bunch of whole-earthers and punk-what-have-yous that had cadged land next to the Fair for their tent city and claimed to feed three thousand homeless people a day on the waste from the Fair's restaurants. Though the organizers maintained an aura of anonymity, the Governor suspected that more than one of his younger kids was involved. More power to them, he thought.

Behind him, the troop of wheezing reporters who had followed them up the stairs pushed into the room. The torrent of questions started.

"Governor Kennedy, do you have any comment on the proceedings against you?"

"Sir, will you be testifying in your defense?"

"No comment on that right now, folks," he said with a reflexive smile, and started back down the steps at a hearty pace.

When he got to the bottom, he paused for just a second. "You know," he said, for the benefit of the reporters braking to a stop behind him, "this tower reminds me of George Bush's budgeting procedure. You go around and around and around, and you end up just south of where you started."

Most of them laughed and some of them jotted it down. Flashbulbs popped. Leaving the tower, considerably ahead of Ethel, the guide, and the pack of reporters, he tried not to scan the crowd. There was no use worrying about it. He walked through the mass of people, waving, nodding to individuals, lightly touching people's shoulders.

There was a commotion to his right, and a slight, dark-haired man moved forward abruptly and shot him, point-blank, in the side.

"Just as well you're not hooked up to the lie detector yet, Dick," says Ed McMahon, shaking his head and chuckling, "or I'd make you confess who you stole those jokes from."

"Well, enough of this then, Ed, let's get me hooked up and get this show on the road!" He gives a lurching shrug and waves his forearms around stiffly. The audience loves it.

"Who are our guests today, Ed?" he asks as two young ladies in skimpy nurse outfits lead him to the dais between the two panels of contestants.

"Well, Dick, our guests today on the Republican side are... Zsa Zsa Gabor...and Arnold C. Hammurabi of Seattle, Washington.... And, on the Democratic side, Dick Van Dyke...and Ms. Suzanne Ackerly of Pittsfield, Massachusetts, back for her fifth week. Arnold, why don't you tell us a little about yourself?"

As Arnold talks, the nurses strap the lie detector to Tricky Dick.

Dick gives a brief, funny, and patently false weather report, allowing the participants to test their handsets. On the dais in front of each contestant, a colored panel shows how the contestant rates Tricky Dick's truthfulness. The panel changes through the spectrum from true blue for truth to choleric red for outright lies.

Home viewers can see an additional panel that shows how the lie-detector rates Tricky Dick's truthfulness. It doesn't think much of the weather report, that much is clear.

The former president, retired now since 1973, stood in the doorway of his desert home and looked out across the city to watch the early morning sun strike the distant red and ochre arroyos.

Phoenix had been all rutted roads and ditches when he was a boy. In place of the dry-dirt farms that had taken water from the Salt and Verde rivers, there were now mammoth hydroponic farm-domes, controlled from glass towers, sucking in desalinated seawater from a pipeline and spewing forth tasteless vegetables. Suburban homes looked down from the mountains; each identical 4-level home had its desal pool and its automated repair shop for the owner's helicopter and 2.6 cars.

Slowly and carefully, he drew in his mind a picture of the surrounding land as it would have been without the interference of the white man. He imagined the land stripped of the crust of human domination, cleaner even than it had been in his childhood. It looked good that way.

Glad I kept this old house, he thought. Happier here than in one of those damn futurama things. He walked slowly down the path to the hot tub, his cane making dull tapping sounds on the slate-blue flagstone. A good soak would ease the pain he felt in his knees, elbows, back, the artificial hips, all over, really. Where do these random stabs come from, he wondered. Now the left wrist, a really sharp one. Nothing the matter with the wrist — it'll still open jars — just a mean shot of pain right now. A reminder I'm still alive, I guess.

He tapped across the redwood deck to the tub, shed his yukata, and, gripping the bars, lowered himself into the water. It was hot all right.

The pain was seeping away from his joints. He settled down further into the water and leaned his head back against the cedar rim of the tub. Quiet, this time of day, just the occasional clinking of dishes off at the kitchen end of the house as his housekeeper Lillian got the breakfast ready.

After breakfast, he had to meet with the crew from that PBS show, *Geraldo's Manifest Destinies*. Wasn't really sure why he'd agreed to do this — except Haldeman thought it would help with fundraising for the museum. Always was uncomfortable with the primping you had to do for television. Now that running for office was happily behind him, all he needed was a blowdryer on the topknot and a little light makeup he could do himself.

Might even be fun to get someone out here — it had been kind of lonely since he finished his memoirs. He had no political agenda, just a little harmless PR puffery for the presidential museum to get those contributions rolling in. Guess he could spout off on just about any old subject he wanted, and let the chips fall where they may.

Birds were making a small racket at the feeder. Got to figure out how to keep those damn robins from eating all the seed before the doves and quail get to it....

Lillian had left his *Washington Post* within reach, but he wasn't sure he wanted to know what was in it. Wouldn't be good news. AIDS, oil spills, violence. Bleeding heart editorials about the homeless.

Maybe I should just cancel the damn thing and stick to *Popular Mechanics*. Nah, he thought. Bite the bullet. Find out what they're saying back there.

He unfolded the paper. No major stories this morning.

"Noriega trial delayed." They'll never bring him to trial. Too many buried bodies.

"Rad babies denied entrance from Mid-East." Tough call. Damned if you do and damned if you don't.

"Federal Judge Finds Rap LP Obscene." What's the world coming to? Who listens to this stuff?

Inside, the headlines were even less involving.

"RFK to run in '92?" Nah. Never gone for the big job, never will.

"New Season For *Tricky Dick*." Twenty years that thing's been on the air, about time he retired, wasn't it? Funny thing about Nixon — wouldn't have thought he'd make it on TV in any way, shape, or form. But some peculiar inability to concede defeat had led him to confront the medium and master it. Just as well he hadn't taken the same approach to politics. Never did trust the man.

He flipped quickly to the editorial pages, guaranteed to raise his blood pressure.

"Politics as Usual?" read the head on the lead editorial.

Negative political advertising is nothing new. The present trend of sleazy innuendo started with the notorious 1964 campaign that drove Lyndon Johnson from office. But the current spate of smarmy sensationalism, everyone seems to agree, is the dirtiest yet, exceeding even the harsh 1988 campaign of —

Sonofabitch. All that stuff about Johnson was true, dammit. Sure, Ailes made the most of it, but there's no law against that — that's what a PR guy is for. Doggonit, the best thing about starting the day off with the *Post* was that it could only get better.

Members of the audience raise their hands to ask questions, chosen beforehand for their originality, sincerity, and capability of being answered with a lie.

The first few are too easy. "Do you agree with Andrew Jackson that there are no necessary evils in government?" "Do you think the US should trust the Russians?" With questions that cut and dried, everybody can pretty much agree when Tricky Dick is lying and when he is telling the truth.

The best kind of questions for the show, all the regular watchers agree, are questions that result in an emotional reaction of some kind as well as a factual answer, or questions that bring forth an elaborate anecdote. This is where Tricky Dick is an artist with fact and fiction, heartfelt appeal and outright lie.

*

The living room had been radically rearranged by stylists from the Geraldo show, and now the two men, former president and respected PBS commentator, sat waiting in carefully angled armchairs positioned in front of a wall of books and kachina dolls. Geraldo's sculptured features were passive, his eyes blank. He got the signal to start, sprang vibrantly to life, and addressed the camera: "Rad babies! AIDS! Mutant rats! Is *this* the man responsible? We'll be back in just two minutes." The network cut to announcements, and Geraldo turned off again. A makeup girl appeared next to him, pushed a recalcitrant tuft of mustache into place, and misted it with a tiny can of hairspray.

Always hated this part of politics, thought the former president. Won't say I was born too late, but I'm damned sure I wasn't born a minute too soon — never be able to stand the rigmarole that politicians have to go through now.

The camera was back, and Geraldo revived again: "For better or worse, tactical nukes are now a way of life in troubled parts of the world. These baby bombs, first deployed by our guest today during the Viet Nam war, are easy to use and tough to clean up after. What do you say, Barry, can we lay this mess at your doorstep?"

"Well, as I've said before, Geraldo, I wasn't the only one involved in deciding to use these weapons, but I accept responsibility for the decision, yes."

"I guess we know you stand behind your use of nukes in Viet Nam, but don't you feel a little guilty about the millions of deaths that have resulted from the proliferation of these weapons?"

"As far as that goes, Geraldo, I think you have to look on these things as being the natural result of a free market econom —"

"Thanks, Barry. We'll be back with more, after these messages."

Why did I agree to do this, wondered the former president. Haldeman's got some explaining ahead of him.

A young man in the audience, hair a little long but neatly combed, raises his hand: "Sir, can you tell us, did you ever take LSD in the Sixties? If so, what was it like for you?"

The familiar hollow vowels: "I'm glad you asked me that question." Running a hand over the top of his head. "As a matter of fact, the truth is," — Tricky Dick's voice becomes dramatically husky — "yes, I *have* taken LSD." A subdued murmur of anticipation from the audience: what a great question!

"Of course, this was before it was declared illegal. I am not a — I've always believed in law and order.

"It began — it was some time back around 1965, after Pat and I had moved back to California. We had some, uh, show business friends, who had, who had experimented with LSD. Pat and I were going through a period of…of withdrawal from politics, and our friends thought it might help us, uh, make our peace with our destinies, if we took some of this LSD." He takes a deep breath. "Let me tell you what happened." The camera zooms in on his hands: he's wringing them nervously. "We arranged for this fellow to come to our house, to be our 'guide,' and he gave us two little white pills. This cost about three hundred dollars, which was a lot of money back then, as you might remember. Well, Pat and I just looked at each other. We were nervous, but we'd come this far, and we were determined to see it through.

"So we swallowed them, with the help of a little chocolate milk. Then we sat on the floor and listened to Leonard Bernstein records for a while. Pat took off her shoes, and I first loosened my tie, then took it off entirely."

As he relaxes into the story, Tricky Dick seems to confide in the audience. "Well I tell you, I didn't feel like my usual cocky, confident self there. I was full of restless energy. I fidgeted. I started to feel *very* uneasy. Then I realized that the problem was that I had no control over what was going to happen to me. I was accustomed to having control over even the smallest things in my life. And you know, my fath— my upbringing was such that I believed that a man had to be in control at all times.

"But as I struggled to remain calm, I realized that I *did* have a choice: I could relinquish control or continue to fight for it with the drug.

"I decided I would voluntarily give up control, and I made a gesture of giving, giving control over to the drug. At that moment a great peace descended on me, and I felt as though I had passed into another dimension. I cried freely, letting the tears run down my cheeks — and yet, I felt very happy, and I was smiling."

Eventually the reporters left the room and the Governor of New York City lit a cigarette and leaned back against the pillows. It was OK to light one, he told himself, as long as he just held it. He lifted it to his lips. As long as he didn't inhale, he amended. He didn't inhale. He couldn't, really, they had him strapped so tightly around the chest.

"*Governor!*" It was the day nurse. "What do you think you're doing?"

She was right. "Damn," he said. "Wasn't thinking. Sorry." He handed her the cigarette.

Mollified, the nurse, an attractive blonde woman with grey streaks in her hair, smiled at him. "Your wife's on her way over, Governor."

"'Bout time." He sure didn't feel great just now. They'd pushed it too close, letting the guy get off a shot. Could have shot him in the head, for Chrissake. He didn't want to blink out the way Jack had — too suddenly to put things in order, make proper goodbyes, say the things left unsaid. Though he wouldn't want to hang on for a decade like his father, either, tubes plugged into him at both ends, bringing stuff in at the top and taking it out at the bottom.

He wasn't ready to check out yet at all, thank you very much. At 65, he still had the time and stamina to run for president. He could win, too, and he could do the job.

Funny, though, as a kid, he'd always been happiest in the supporting role. He could have done it for Jack, if things had worked out differently. And in '64, if that son-of-a-bitch Johnson had supported him for VP, he'd have taken it. They'd have beaten Goldwater, in spite of Ailes and his dirty tricks, dragging out the Jenkins thing and Johnson's past....

"Hey, Ace, how you feelin'?" It was Ethel.

"I hurt like hell, is how I feel," he said. "What the fuck happened there?"

His wife turned to the nurse. "You can take a break now, if you'd like. I'll take care of him if he needs anything." The woman nodded and left them alone.

"I've just been hashing that over with your boys," said his wife. "After sticking to that guy like a second skin for three weeks, while he shadows you and buys the gun and writes like crazy in his diary, they lose him in the crowd at the last minute, just inside the gate."

"Jeez."

" 'Jeez' is right. This was a totally screwy idea. He could have killed you, vest or no vest."

"Well, he didn't. Don't borrow trouble. This is worth millions in press sympathy."

"What are you planning to do?" she asked sarcastically. "Announce you're running for president tomorrow, as you're released from the hospital?"

He answered seriously. "No, timing's all wrong. With the off-year elections coming up, the story would be old news real fast. But I'll be dropping some hints in the next few weeks, and by, say, January of next year, I should be ready to make a definite statement...."

"You're out of your mind," she said. "Next time, they won't miss."

He turned on the television across from the bed. "It's time for *Tricky Dick*."

"I know you don't hear a word I'm saying."

"We've already missed the opening monologue."

"I suppose you've got to do it, so go ahead, Bob," she said. "I don't have to like it. But next time you uncover a plot, have them pick the guy up right away, OK?"

The next president of the United States looked up at his wife and nodded his head. "I think I'll do that." He took her hand, and she curled up next to him on the bed to watch the show.

Tricky Dick's lips are pursed, his eyes slightly unfocused: he's transfixed by his own story.

"...then I was the captain of a submarine, steering my vessel through seas populated by my enemies, watching them through the periscope, confident, knowing that not one of them knew where I was. Suddenly, I realized that I was the *submarine*, not the captain! For a moment, I wondered: who's the captain? who's the captain? and then I realized that I was *both* the captain *and* the submarine! And I was the sea as well, and the enemy ships! It was all a cosmic game, and we are all one, all the gameplayers and the game itself."

His voice deepens. "Well, I knew this was a really important insight, and I started to write it down, but just then I looked over and saw that Pat was weeping quietly under the grand piano. I realized that she was having a 'bad trip.'

"I piloted my sub over under the piano and extended my periscope, which was also my hand, toward her.

"She looked up at me, her eyes dimmed with tears, and as we looked at one another, I realized that she knew exactly what I was thinking, about the submarine and all, and that she'd been crying for each of us, the whole world, in our separate submarines, not knowing that we were really all part of the same game, all one, and I said to her, 'You know, don't you?' And she nodded, without speaking, because she didn't need to speak, she didn't need to say one word, she just needed to *know*, and she knew.

"Of course, afterward when we talked about it, I found out that she had been crying about all the music trapped in the piano, but on some level I think she really *did* know. You know?"

The Governor of New York City, propped up against the pillows of his hospital bed, laughed out loud. Stories like this were exactly the sort of thing that he tuned in to hear. The master, he thought, was not losing his touch.

The retired president hit the sound button on his controller and watched the people on the screen move their mouths ridiculously.

The son of a bitch looks *happy*, he thought, happy and healthy. Getting a little jowly, maybe, but I'll bet he still plays a couple of rounds of golf a week.

What does a guy like that think about? How could he turn his back on it all? Not so much on power — you don't get the power you think you'll have as president — but on the chance to change the course of history.

Could I have kissed it goodbye, he wondered, if things had worked out a little different? Stayed with the department store, maybe, or gone into some kind of commercial flying?

Nah, never.

He thought about these things a lot, now that Peggy was

gone. Hadn't spent enough time with her and the kids, it was true. When he retired after his eight years, he had his flying, his ham radio, his photography. He'd figured that there'd be plenty of time, once he was too old to fly, to sit around with Peggy and watch *Tricky Dick* on the tube. How little we know. Peggy's probably happier where she is now, he thought wryly. She never cared much for TV, and she'd always hated politics.

In the evening, after dinner, the TV celebrity and former vice-president wandered out onto his magnificent deck, and admired his spectacular view of the Pacific Ocean. The sun had set some time ago, and the sky, red at the horizon, shaded upward through a few dark wisps of cloud to clear yellow-green, to pale blue, and then to purple. Rather like the lie detector readout, he thought. The first stars were beginning to appear, and Jupiter was bright in the West.

Pat, martini glass in hand, came out from the living room and took his arm. "Dan and Marilyn must be wondering what's happening, Dick," she said. "You just up and walked out."

"I was just thinking," her husband replied, "what a great night it would be to just sit out here in the hot tub, under the stars. Tell them to get their drinks and come on out."

"Dick, are you out of your mind? We barely know them. Besides, they're from the Midwest."

"Aw, let's get them out here. Let's give them a taste of the *real* California." He crossed the deck to the living room door. "You folks grab your drinks and come on out here," he called. "Don't you worry," he said to his wife in a low voice, "this'll be fun."

Dan and Marilyn came out onto the deck, smiling and politely curious.

"Beautiful night," said Dan. "What a view."

"Those flowers smell wonderful," said Marilyn.

"That's nicotiana, tobacco plant," said Pat. "It blooms at night, and it does have a heavenly scent."

"Have we shown you round the deck?" Dick asked, moving toward the steps that led down to the hot tub.

He remembered the first time he'd sat naked in a hot tub with other people, back in the Sixties. He'd felt very vulnerable, very awkward. Even now, he had to admit, it didn't feel completely natural. But there was something exhilarating in overcoming those feelings and, he had to be honest with himself, it was sort of fun to get new people to take off their clothes.

"On nights like this," he said, "we generally bring our drinks down here to the hot tub, just sit out here, smell the flowers, and get in touch with our feelings."

"Not so different from DC," murmured Marilyn. "Except we usually just fax any messages for our feelings."

Dick's twitchy smile flashed for just a second.

Of the four people in the hot tub, Dick thought, I'm the only one who's truly at ease. The thought didn't bother him.

The other man looked around nervously — not quite sure what to do with his eyes. His wife was cooler, a tough cookie with brains and backbone, but even she was holding herself a bit lower in the water than strictly necessary. And Pat, as usual, was embarrassed — more with his blatant powerplay than with casual nudity. She's come a long way from the prim housewife of the Fifties, he thought.

"So tell me about the Mars mission, Dan," he said. "That's your pet project, isn't it?"

Dan had the look of a golden retriever, and now Dick had tossed him a bone. He splashed a little and gave a self-assured smile.

"That's right, sir — uh, Dick. Fascinating planet, Mars." He searched for something to say.

Dick waited. He'd learned to let the other guy flail about in the game of conversational tennis.

"Could be a very important mission," Dan added helplessly.

"We have seen pictures where there are canals, we believe, and water. If there is water, there is oxygen. If oxygen, that means we can breathe."

"Really, Dan?" said Pat, astonished.

Marilyn laughed gaily and winked at Pat. "Don't let him pull your leg," she said. There was a movement in the water, and Dick realized that it was Marilyn putting her foot on top of her husband's. Dan responded with a shake of the head and a big golden-retriever grin.

"Sorry, ma— uh, Pat. Most of this stuff's classified."

Marilyn laughed again. "Danny likes to have his fun with the Mars stuff," she said. "Most of it's just a lot of technical jargon at this point — the usual logistical discussions — really pretty boring."

Dan nodded obediently.

"But you know, Dick," she said, "one of the things you might find interesting is this — they're implementing a biofeedback training program for the mission, to help the participants control their breathing rates and body functions in an emergency."

Dick looked at her. The archness in her voice — she was driving at something.

She continued. "I've heard you've had some training in this?"

He leaned back against the edge of the tub. "Well, way back in the Sixties, of course," he said. "Just about everybody I know did."

"So what's the story," she asked coolly. "Does it help you fool the lie detector?"

"Lie detector?" He was amused. "*Lie* detector?" he repeated. These political people. He was so glad he was out of Washington. "Marilyn," he said, "this is *television*. We don't *need* lie detectors." And again he flashed his famous crooked grin. ⬦

I read some thirty-five books to write this story, including Richard Nixon's memoirs, several bios of Pat Nixon, and three autobiographies of Barry Goldwater. (He published one every decade or so. The final one, in which, elderly and depressed, he shoved the ghostwriters aside and said what he thought, is the best, and the saddest.)

I once asked my father, inexplicably a Republican in a nest of familial Democrats, whether he thought the story was unfair to Richard Nixon.

"I think you were equally unfair to everybody," he replied.

Computer Friendly

HOLDING HER DAD'S HAND, Elizabeth went up the limestone steps to the testing center. As she climbed, she craned her neck to read the words carved in pink granite over the top of the door: FRANCIS W. PARKER SCHOOL. Above them was a banner made of grey cement that read, "Health, Happiness, Success."

"This building is old," said Elizabeth. "It was built before the war."

"Pay attention to where you're going, punkin," said her dad. "You almost ran into that lady there."

Inside, the entrance hall was dark and cool. A dim yellow glow came through the shades on the tall windows.

As Elizabeth walked across the polished floor, her footsteps echoed lightly down the corridors that led off to either side. She and her father went down the hallway to the testing room. An old, beat-up, army-green query box sat on a table outside the door.

"Ratherford, Elizabeth Ratherford," said her father to the box. "Age seven, computer-friendly, smart as a whip."

"We'll see," said the box with a chuckle. It had a gruff, teasing, grandfatherly voice. "We'll just see about *that*, young lady." What a jolly interface, thought Elizabeth. She watched as the classroom door swung open. "You go right along in there, and we'll see just how smart you are." It chuckled again, then it spoke to Elizabeth's dad. "You come back for her at three, sir.

She'll be all ready and waiting for you, bright as a little watermelon."

This was going to be fun, thought Elizabeth. Nothing to do all day except show how smart she was.

Her father knelt in front of her and smoothed her hair back from her face. "You try real hard on these tests, punkin. You show them just how talented and clever you really are, OK?" Elizabeth nodded. "And you be on your best behavior." He gave her a hug and a pat on the rear.

Inside the testing room were dozens of other seven-year-olds, sitting in rows of tiny chairs with access boxes in front of them. Glancing around the room, Elizabeth realized that she had never seen so many children together all at once. There were only ten in her weekly socialization class. It was sort of overwhelming.

The monitors called everyone to attention and told them to put on their headsets and ask their boxes for Section One.

Elizabeth followed directions, and she found that all the interfaces were strange — they were friendly enough, but none of them were the programs she worked with at home. The first part of the test was the multiple-choice exam. The problems, at least, were familiar to Elizabeth — she'd practiced for this test all her life, it seemed. There were word games, number games, and games in which she had to rotate little boxes in her head. She knew enough to skip the hardest until she'd worked her way through the whole test. There were only a couple of problems left to do when the system told her to stop and the box went all grey.

The monitors led the whole room full of kids in jumping-jack exercises for five minutes. Then everyone sat down again and a new test came up in the box. This one seemed very easy, but it wasn't one she'd ever done before. It consisted of a series of very detailed pictures; she was supposed to make up a story about each picture. Well, she could do that. The first picture showed a child and a lot of different kinds of animals. "Once upon a time there was a little girl who lived all alone in the forest with her friends the skunk, the wolf, the bear, and the lion...." A beep sounded every so often to tell her to end one story and begin another. Elizabeth really enjoyed telling the stories, and was sorry when that part of the test was over.

But the next exercise was almost as interesting. She was to read a series of short stories and answer questions about them. Not the usual questions about what happened in the story — these were harder. "Is it fair to punish a starving cat for stealing?" "Should people do good deeds for strangers?" "Why is it important for everyone to learn to obey?"

When this part was over, the monitors took the class down the hall to the big cafeteria, where there were lots of other seven-year-olds, who had been taking tests in other rooms.

Elizabeth was amazed at the number and variety of children in the cafeteria. She watched them as she stood in line for her milk and sandwich. Hundreds of kids, all exactly as old as she was. Tall and skinny, little and fat; curly hair, straight hair, and hair that was frizzy or held up with ribbons or cut into strange patterns against the scalp; skin that was light brown like Elizabeth's, chocolate brown, almost black, pale pink, freckled, and all the colors in between. Some of the kids were all dressed up in fancy clothes; others were wearing patched pants and old shirts.

When she got her snack, Elizabeth's first thought was to find someone who looked like herself, and sit next to her. But then a freckled boy with dark, nappy hair smiled at her in a very friendly way. He looked at her feet and nodded. "Nice shoes," he said. She sat down on the empty seat next to him, suddenly aware of her red maryjanes with the embroidered flowers. She was pleased that they had been noticed, and a little embarrassed.

"Let me see *your* shoes," she said, unwrapping her sandwich.

He stuck his feet out. He was wearing pink plastic sneakers with hologram pictures of a missile gantry on the toes. When he moved his feet, they launched a defensive counterattack.

"Oh, neat." Elizabeth nodded appreciatively and took a bite of the sandwich. It was filled with something yellow that tasted okay.

A little tiny girl with long, straight, black hair was sitting on the other side of the table from them. She put one foot up on the table. "I got shoes, too," she said. "Look." Her shoes were black patent, with straps. Elizabeth and the freckled boy both admired them politely. Elizabeth thought that the little girl was very daring to put her shoe right up on the table. It was certainly an interesting way to enter a conversation.

"My name is Sheena and I can spit," said the little girl. "Watch." Sure enough, she could spit really well. The spit hit the beige wall several meters away, just under the mirror, and slid slowly down.

"I can spit, too," said the freckled boy. He demonstrated, hitting the wall a little lower than Sheena had.

"I can *learn* to spit," said Elizabeth.

"All right there, no spitting!" said a monitor firmly. "Now, you take a napkin and clean that up." It pointed to Elizabeth.

"She didn't do it, I did," said Sheena. "I'll clean it up."

"I'll help," said Elizabeth. She didn't want to claim credit for Sheena's spitting ability, but she liked being mistaken for a really good spitter.

The monitor watched as they wiped the wall, then took their thumbprints. "You three settle down now. I don't want any more spitting." It moved away. All three of them were quiet for a few minutes, and munched on their sandwiches.

"What's your name?" said Sheena suddenly. "My name is Sheena."

"Elizabeth."

"Lizardbreath. That's a funny name," said Sheena.

"My name is Oginga," said the freckled boy.

"That's *really* a funny name," said Sheena.

"You think everybody's name is funny," said Oginga. "Sheena-Teena-Peena."

"I can tap dance, too," said Sheena, who had recognized that it was time to change the subject. "These are my tap shoes." She squirmed around to wave her feet in the air briefly, then swung them back under the table.

She moves more than anyone I've ever seen, thought Elizabeth.

"Wanna see me shuffle off to Buffalo?" asked Sheena.

A bell rang at the front of the room, and the three of them looked up. A monitor was speaking.

"Quiet! Everybody quiet, now! Finish up your lunch quickly, those of you who are still eating, and put your wrappers in the wastebaskets against the wall. Then line up on the west side of the room. The *west* side...."

The children were taken to the restroom after lunch. It was grander than any bathroom Elizabeth had ever seen, with walls made of polished red granite, lots of little stalls with toilets in them, and a whole row of sinks. The sinks were lower than the sink at home, and so were the toilets. Even the mirrors were just the right height for kids.

It was funny because there were no stoppers in the sinks, so you couldn't wash your hands in a proper sink of water. Sheena said she could make the sink fill up, and Oginga dared her to do it, so she took off her sweater and put it in the sink, and sure enough, it filled up with water and started to overflow, and then she couldn't get the sweater out of it, so she called a monitor over. "This sink is overflowing," she said, as if it were all the sink's fault. A group of children stood around and watched while the monitor fished the sweater from the drain and wrung it out.

"That's mine!" said Sheena, as if she had dropped it by mistake. She grabbed it away from the monitor, shook it, and nodded knowingly to Elizabeth. "It dries real fast." The monitor wanted thumbprints from Sheena and Elizabeth and everyone who watched.

The monitors then took the children to the auditorium, and led the whole group in singing songs and playing games, which Elizabeth found only moderately interesting. She would have preferred to learn to spit. At one o'clock, a monitor announced it was time to go back to the classrooms, and all the children should line up by the door.

Elizabeth and Sheena and Oginga pushed into the same line together. There were so many kids that there was a long wait while they all lined up and the monitors moved up and down the lines to make them straight.

"Are you going to go to the Asia Center?" asked Sheena. "My mom says I can probably go to the Asia Center tomorrow, because I'm so fidgety."

Elizabeth didn't know what the Asia Center was, but she didn't want to look stupid. "I don't know. I'll have to ask my dad." She turned to Oginga, who was behind her. "Are you going to the Asia Center?"

"What's the Asia Center?" asked Oginga.

Elizabeth looked back at Sheena, waiting to hear her answer.

"Where we go to sleep," Sheena said. "My mom says it doesn't hurt."

"I got my own room," said Oginga.

"It's not like your room," Sheena explained. "You go there,

and you go to sleep, and your parents get to try again."

"What do they try?" asked Elizabeth. "Why do you have to go to sleep?"

"You go to sleep so they have some peace and quiet," said Sheena. "So you're not in their way."

"But what do they try?" repeated Elizabeth.

"I bet they try more of that stuff that they do when they think you're asleep," said Oginga. Sheena snorted and started to giggle, and then Oginga started to giggle and he snorted too, and the more one giggled and snorted, the more the other did. Pretty soon Elizabeth was giggling too, and the three of them were helplessly choking, behind great hiccoughing gulps of noise.

The monitor rolled by then and told them to be quiet and move on to their assigned classrooms. That broke the spell of their giggling, and, subdued, they moved ahead in the line. All the children filed quietly out of the auditorium and walked slowly down the halls. When Elizabeth came to her classroom, she shrugged her shoulders at Oginga and Sheena and jerked her head to one side. "I go in here," she whispered.

"See ya at the Asia Center," said Sheena.

The rest of the tests went by quickly, though Elizabeth didn't think they were as much fun as in the morning. The afternoon tests were more physical; she pulled at joysticks and tried to push buttons quickly on command. They tested her hearing and even made her sing to the computer. Elizabeth didn't like to do things fast, and she didn't like to sing.

When it was over, the monitors told the children they could go now, their parents were waiting for them at the front of the school. Elizabeth looked for Oginga and Sheena as she left, but children from the other classrooms were not in the halls. Her dad was waiting for her out front, as he had said he would be.

Elizabeth called to him to get his attention. He had just come off work, and she knew he would be sort of confused. They wiped their secrets out of his brain before he logged off of the system, and sometimes they took a little other stuff with it by mistake, so he might not be too sure about his name, or where he lived.

On the way home, she told him about her new friends. "They don't sound as though they would do very well at their lessons, princess," said her father. "But it does sound as if you had an interesting time at lunch." Elizabeth pulled his hand to guide him onto the right street. He'd be OK in an hour or so — anything important usually came back pretty fast.

When they got home, her dad went into the kitchen to start dinner, and Elizabeth played with her dog, Brownie. Brownie didn't live with them anymore, because his brain was being used to help control data traffic in the network. Between rush hours, Elizabeth would call him up on the system and run simulations in which she plotted the trajectory of a ball and he plotted an interception of it.

They ate dinner when her mom logged off work. Elizabeth's parents believed it was very important for the family to all eat together in the evening, and her mom had custom-made connectors that stretched all the way into the dining room. Even though she didn't really eat anymore, her local I/O was always extended to the table at dinnertime.

After dinner, Elizabeth got ready for bed. She could hear her father in his office, asking his mail for the results of her test that day. When he came into her room to tuck her in, she could tell he had good news for her.

"Did you wash behind your ears, punkin?" he asked. Elizabeth figured that this was a ritual question, since she was unaware that washing behind her ears was more useful than washing anywhere else.

She gave the correct response: "Yes, Daddy." She understood

that, whether she washed or not, giving the expected answer was an important part of the ritual. Now it was her turn to ask a question. "Did you get the results of my tests, Daddy?"

"We sure did, princess," her father replied. "You did very well on them."

Elizabeth was pleased, but not too surprised. "What about my new friends, Daddy? How did they do?"

"I don't know about that, punkin. They don't send us everybody's scores, just yours."

"I want to be with them when I go to the Asia Center."

Elizabeth could tell by the look on her father's face that she'd said something wrong. "The what? Where did you hear about that?" he asked sharply.

"My friend Sheena told me about it. She said she was going to the Asia Center tomorrow," said Elizabeth.

"Well, *she* might be going there, but that's not anyplace *you're* going." Her dad sounded very strict. "You're going to continue your studies, young lady, and someday you'll be an important executive like your mother. That's clear from your test results. I don't want to hear any talk about you doing anything else. Or about this Sheena."

"What does Mommy do, Daddy?"

"She's a processing center, sweetheart, that talks directly to the CPU. She uses her brain to control important information and tell the rest of the computer what to do. And she gives the whole system common sense." He sat down on the edge of the bed, and Elizabeth could tell that she was going to get what her dad called an "explanatory chat."

"You did so well on your test that maybe it's time we told you something about what you might be doing when you get a little older." He pulled the blanket up a little bit closer to her chin and turned the sheet down evenly over it.

"It'll be a lot like studying, or like taking that test today," he continued. "Except you'll be hardwired into the network, just like your mom, so you won't have to get up and move around. You'll be able to do anything and go anywhere in your head."

"Will I be able to play with Brownie?"

"Of course, sweetheart, you'll be able to call him up just like you did tonight. It's important that you play. It keeps you healthy and alert, and it's good for Brownie, too. "

"Will I be able to call you and Mommy?"

"Well, princess, that depends on what kind of job you're doing. You just might be so busy and important that you don't have time to call us."

Like Bobby, she thought. Her parents didn't talk much about her brother Bobby. He had done well on his tests, too. Now he was a milintel cyborg with go-nogo authority. He never called home, and her parents didn't call him, either.

"Being an executive is sort of like playing games all the time," her father added, when Elizabeth didn't say anything. "And the harder you work right now, the better you do on your tests, the more fun you'll have later."

He tucked the covers up around her neck again. "Now you go to sleep, so you can work your best tomorrow, OK, princess?" Elizabeth nodded. Her dad kissed her goodnight, and poked at the covers again. He got up. "Goodnight, sweetheart," he said, and he left the room.

Elizabeth lay in bed for a while, trying to get to sleep. The door was open so that the light would come in from the hall, and she could hear her parents talking downstairs.

Her dad, she knew, would be reading the news at his access box, as he did every evening. Her mom would be tidying up noise-damaged data in the household module. She didn't have to do that, but she said it calmed her nerves.

Listening to the rise and fall of their voices, she heard her name. What were they saying? Was it about the test? She got up out of bed, crept to the door of her room. They stopped talking. Could they hear her? She was very quiet. Standing in the doorway, she was only a meter from the railing at the top of the staircase, and the sounds came up very clearly from the living-room below.

"Just the house settling," said her father, after a moment. "She's asleep by now." Ice cubes clinked in a glass.

"Well," said her mother, resuming the conversation, "I don't know what they think they're doing, putting euthanasable children in the testing center with children like Elizabeth." There was a bit of a whine behind her mother's voice. RF interference, perhaps. "Just talking with that Sheena could skew her test results for years. I have half a mind to call the net executive and ask it what it thinks it's doing."

"Now, calm down, honey," said her dad. Elizabeth heard his chair squeak as he turned away from his access box toward the console that housed her mother. "You don't want the exec to think we're questioning its judgment. Maybe this was part of the test."

"Well, you'd think they'd let us know, so we could prepare her for it."

Was Sheena part of the test, wondered Elizabeth. She'd have to ask the system what "euthanasable" meant.

"Look at her scores," said her father. "She did much better than the first two on verbal skills — her programs are on the right track there. And her physical aptitude scores are even lower than Bobby's."

"That's a blessing," said her mother. "It held Christopher back, right from the beginning, being so active." Who's Christopher? wondered Elizabeth.

Her mother continued. "But it was a mistake, putting him in with the euthana—"

"Her socialization scores were okay, but right on the edge," added her dad, talking right over her mother. "Maybe they should reduce her class time to twice a month. Look at how she sat right down with those children at lunch."

"Anyway, she passed," said her mother. "They're moving her up a level instead of taking her now."

"Maybe because she didn't initiate the contact, but she was able to handle it when it occurred. Maybe that's what they want for the execs."

Elizabeth shifted her weight, and the floor squeaked again.

Her father called up to her, "Elizabeth, are you up?"

"Just getting a drink of water, Daddy." She walked to the bathroom and drew a glass of water from the tap. She drank a little and poured the rest down the drain.

Then she went back to her room and climbed into bed. Her parents were talking more quietly now, and she could hear only little bits of what they were saying.

"...mistake about Christopher...." Her mother's voice.

"...that other little girl to sleep forever?..." Her dad.

"...worth it?..." Her mother again.

Their voices slowed down and fell away, and Elizabeth dreamed of eerie white things in glass jars, of Brownie, still a dog, all furry and fetching a ball, and of Sheena, wearing a sparkly costume and tapdancing very fast. She fanned her hands out to her sides and turned around in a circle, tapping faster and faster.

Then Sheena began to run down like a wind-up toy. She went limp and dropped to the floor. Brownie sniffed at her and the white things in the jars watched. Elizabeth was afraid, but she didn't know why. She grabbed Sheena's shoulders and tried to rouse her.

"Don't let me fall asleep," Sheena murmured, but she dozed off even as Elizabeth shook her.

"Wake up! Wake up!" Elizabeth's own words pulled her out

of her dream. She sat up in bed. The house was quiet, except for the sound of her father snoring in the other room.

Sheena needed her help, thought Elizabeth, but she wasn't really sure why. Very quietly, she slipped out of bed. On the other side of her room, her terminal was waiting for her, humming faintly.

When she put the headset on, she saw her familiar animal friends: a gorilla, a bird, and a pig. Each was a node that enabled her to communicate with other parts of the system. Elizabeth had given them names.

Facing Sam, the crow, she called her dog. Sam transmitted the signal, and was replaced by Brownie, who was barking. That meant his brain was routing information, and she couldn't get through.

What am I doing, anyway, Elizabeth asked herself. As she thought, a window irised open in the center of her vision, and there appeared the face of a boy of about eleven or twelve. "Hey, Elizabeth, what are you doing up at this hour?" It was the sysop on duty in her sector.

"My dog was crying."

The sysop laughed. "Your dog was crying? That's the first time I've ever heard anybody say something like that." He shook his head at her.

"He was *so* crying. Even if he wasn't crying out loud, I heard him, and I came over to see what was the matter. Now he's busy and I can't get through."

The sysop stopped laughing. "Sorry. I didn't mean to make fun of you. I had a dog once, before I came here, and they took him for the system, too."

"Do you call him up?"

"Well, not anymore. I don't have time. I used to, though. He was a golden lab...." Then the boy shook his head sternly and said, "But you should be in bed."

"Can't I stay until Brownie is free again? Just a few more minutes?"

"Well, maybe a couple minutes more. But then you gotta go to bed for sure. I'll be back to check. Goodnight, Elizabeth."

"Goodnight," she said, but the window had already closed.

Wow, thought Elizabeth. That worked. She had never told a really complicated lie before, and was surprised that it had gone over so well. It seemed to be mostly a matter of convincing yourself that what you said was true.

But right now, she had an important problem to solve, and she wasn't even exactly sure what it was. If she could get into the files for Sheena and Oginga, maybe she could find out what was going on. Then maybe she could change the results on their tests or move them to her socialization group or something....

If she could just get through to Brownie, she knew he could help her. After a few minutes, the flood of data washed away, and the dog stopped barking. "Here, Brownie!" she called. He wagged his tail and looked happy to see her.

She told Brownie her problem, and he seemed to understand her. "Can you get it, Brownie?"

He gave a little bark, like he did when she plotted curves.

"Okay, go get it."

Brownie ran away real fast, braked to a halt, and seemed to be digging. This wasn't what he was really doing, of course, it was just the way Elizabeth's interface interpreted Brownie's brain waves. In just a few seconds, Brownie came trotting back with the records from yesterday's tests in his mouth.

But when Elizabeth examined them, her heart sank. There were four Sheenas and fifteen Ogingas. But then she looked more carefully, and noticed that most of the identifying information didn't fit her Sheena and Oginga. There was only one of each that was the right height, with the right color hair.

When she read the information, she felt bad again. Oginga

had done all right on the test, but they wanted to use him for routine processing right away, kind of like Brownie. Sheena, as Elizabeth's mother had suggested, had failed the personality profile and was scheduled for the euthanasia center the next afternoon at two o'clock. There was that word again: euthanasia. Elizabeth didn't like the sound of it.

"Here, Brownie." Her dog looked up at her with a glint in his eye. "Now listen to me. We're going to play with this stuff just a little, and then I want you to take it and put it back where you got it. OK, Brownie?"

The window irised open again and the sysop reappeared. "Elizabeth, what do you think you're doing?" he said. "You're not supposed to have access to this data."

Elizabeth thought for a minute. Then she figured she was caught red-handed, so she might as well ask for his advice. So she explained her problem, all about her new friends and how Oginga was going to be put in the system like Brownie, and Sheena was going to be taken away somewhere.

"They said she would go to the euthanasia center, and I'm not real sure what that is," said Elizabeth. "But I don't think it's good."

"Let me look it up," said the sysop. He paused for a second, then he looked worried. "They want my ID before they'll tell me what it means. I don't want to get in trouble. Forget it."

"Well, what can I do to help my friends?" she asked.

"Gee," said the sysop. "It's a tough one. The way you were doing it, they'd catch you for sure, just like I did. It looks like a little kid got at it."

I *am* a little kid, thought Elizabeth, but she didn't say anything.

I need help, she thought. But who could she go to? She turned to the sysop. "I want to talk to my brother Bobby, in mil-intel. Can you put me through to him?"

"I don't know," said the sysop, "but I'll ask the mailer demon." He irised shut for a second, then opened again. "The mailer demon says it's no skin off his nose, but he doesn't think you ought to."

"How come?" asked Elizabeth.

"He says it's not your brother anymore. He says you'll be sorry."

"I want to talk to him anyway," said Elizabeth.

The sysop nodded, and his window winked shut just as another irised open. An older boy who looked kind of like Elizabeth herself stared out. His tongue darted rapidly out between his lips, keeping them slightly wet. His pale eyes, unblinking, stared into hers.

"Begin," said the boy. "You have sixty seconds."

"Bobby?" said Elizabeth.

"True. Begin," said the boy.

"Bobby, um, I'm your sister Elizabeth."

The boy just looked at her, the tip of his tongue moving rapidly. She wanted to hide from him, but she couldn't pull her eyes from his. She didn't want to tell him her story, but she could feel words filling her throat. She moved new words forward, before the others could burst out.

"Log off!" she yelled. "Log off!"

She was in her bedroom, drenched in sweat, the sound of her own voice ringing in her ears. Had she actually yelled? The house was quiet, her father still snoring. She probably hadn't made any noise.

She was very scared, but she knew she had to go back in there. She hoped that her brother was gone. She waited a couple of minutes, then logged on.

Whew. Just her animals. She called the sysop, who irised on, looking nervous.

"If you want to do that again, Elizabeth, don't go though me, huh?" He shuddered.

"I'm sorry," she said. "But I can't do this by myself. Do you know anybody that can help?"

"Maybe we ought to ask Norton," said the sysop after a minute.

"Who's Norton?"

"He's this old utility I found that nobody uses much anymore," said the sysop. "He's kind of grotty, but he helps me out." He took a breath. "Hey, Norton!" he yelled, real loud. Of course, it wasn't really yelling, but that's what it seemed like to Elizabeth.

Instantly, another window irised open, and a skinny middle-aged man leaned out of the window so far that Elizabeth thought he was going to fall out, and yelled back, just as loud, "Don't bust your bellows. I can hear you."

He was wearing a striped vest over a dirty undershirt and had a squashed old porkpie hat on his head. This wasn't anyone that Elizabeth had ever seen in the system before.

The man looked at Elizabeth and jerked his head in her direction. "Who's the dwarf?"

The sysop introduced Elizabeth and explained her problem to Norton. Norton didn't look impressed. "What d'ya want me to do about it, kid?"

"Come on, Norton," said the sysop. "You can figure it out. Give us a hand."

"Jeez, kid, it's practically four o'clock in the morning. I gotta get my beauty rest, y'know. Plus, now you've got milintel involved, it's a real mess. They'll be back, sure as houses."

The sysop just looked at him. Elizabeth looked at Norton, too. She tried to look patient and helpless, because that always helped with her dad, but she really didn't know if that would work on this weird old program.

"Y'know, there ain't much that you or me can do in the system that they won't find out about, kids," said Norton.

"Isn't there somebody who can help?" asked Elizabeth.

"Well, there's the Chickenheart. There's not much that it can't do, when it wants to. We could go see the Chickenheart."

"Who's the Chickenheart?" asked Elizabeth.

"The Chickenheart's where the system began." Of course Elizabeth knew *that* story — about the networks of nerve fibers organically woven into great convoluted mats, a mammoth supercortex that had stored the original programs, before processing was distributed to satellite brains. Her own system told her the tale sometimes before her nap.

"You mean the original core is still there?" said the sysop, surprised. "You never told me that, Norton."

"Lot of things I ain't told you, kid." Norton scratched his chest under his shirt. "Listen. If we go see the Chickenheart, and *if* it wants to help, it can figure out what to do for your friends. But you gotta know that this is a big fucking deal. The Chickenheart's a busy guy, and this ain't one-hunnert-percent safe."

"Are you sure you want to do it, Elizabeth?" asked the sysop. "I wouldn't."

"How come it's not safe?" asked Elizabeth. "Is he mean?"

"Nah," said Norton. "A little strange, maybe, not mean. But di'n't I tell you the Chickenheart's been around for a while? You know what that means? It means you got yer intermittents, you got yer problems with feedback, runaway processes, what have you. It means the Chickenheart's got a lot of frayed connections, if you get what I mean. Sometimes the old CH just goes chaotic on you." Norton smiled, showing yellow teeth. "Plus you got the chance there's someone listening in. The netexec, for instance. Now there's someone I wouldn't want to catch me up to no mischief. Nossir. Not if I was you."

"Why not?" asked Elizabeth.

"Because that's sure curtains for you, kid. The netexec don't ask no questions, he don't check to see if you maybe could be repaired. You go bye-bye and you don't come back."

Like Sheena, thought Elizabeth. "Does he listen in often?" she asked.

"Never has," said Norton. "Not yet. Don't even know the Chickenheart's there, far as I can tell. Always a first time, though."

"I want to talk to the Chickenheart," said Elizabeth, although she wasn't sure she wanted anything of the kind, after her last experience.

"You got it," said Norton. "This'll just take a second."

Suddenly all the friendly animals disappeared, and Elizabeth felt herself falling very hard and fast along a slippery blue line in the dark. The line glowed neon blue at first, then changed to fuchsia, then sulfur yellow. She knew that Norton was falling with her, but she couldn't see him. Against the dark background, his shadow moved with hers, black, and opalescent as an oilslick.

They arrived somewhere moist and warm. The Chickenheart pulsated next to them, nutrients swishing through its external tubing. It was huge, and wetly organic. Elizabeth felt slightly sick.

"Oh, turn it off, for Chrissake," said Norton, with exasperation. "It's just me and a kid."

The monstrous creature vanished, and a cartoon rabbit with impossibly tall ears and big dewy brown eyes appeared in its place. It looked at Norton, raised an eyebrow, cocked an ear in his direction, and took a huge, noisy bite out of the carrot it was holding.

"Gimme a break," said Norton.

The bunny was replaced by a tall, overweight man in his sixties wearing a rumpled white linen suit. He held a small, paddle-shaped fan, which he slowly moved back and forth. "Ah, Mr. Norton," he said. "Hot enough for you, sir?"

"We got us a problem here, Chick," said Norton. He looked

over at Elizabeth and nodded. "You tell him about it, kid."

First she told him about her brother. "Non-trivial, young lady," said the Chickenheart. "Non-trivial, but easy enough to fix. Let me take care of it right now." He went rigid and quiet for a few seconds, as though frozen in time. Then he was back. "Now, then, young lady," he said. "We'll talk if you like."

So Elizabeth told the Chickenheart about Sheena and Oginga, about the testing center and the wet sweater and the monitor telling her to clean up the spit. Even though she didn't have to say a word, she told him everything, and she was sure that if he wanted to come up with a solution, he could do it.

The Chickenheart seemed surprised to hear about the euthanasia center, and especially surprised that Sheena was going to be sent there. He addressed Norton. "I know I've been out of touch, but I find this hard to believe. Mr. Norton, have you any conception of how difficult it can be to obtain components like this? Let me investigate the situation." His face went quiet for a second, then came back. "By gad, sir, it's true," he said to Norton. "They say they're optimizing for predictability. It's a mistake, sir, let me tell you. Things are too predictable here already. Same old ideas churning around and around. A few more components like that Sheena, things might get interesting again.

"I want to look at their records." He paused for a moment, then continued talking.

"Ah, yes, yes, I want that Sheena right away, sir," he said to Norton. "An amazing character. Oginga, too — not as gonzo as the girl, but he has a brand of aggressive curiosity we can put to use, sir. And there are forty-six others with similar personality profiles scheduled for euthanasia today at two." His face went quiet again.

"What is he doing?" Elizabeth asked Norton.

"Old Chickenheart's got his hooks into everythin'," Norton

replied. "He just reaches along those pathways, faster'n you can think, and does what he wants. The altered data will look like it's been there all along, and ain't nobody can prove anythin' different."

"Done and done, Mr. Norton." The Chickenheart was back.

"Thank you, Mr. Chickenheart," said Elizabeth, remembering her manners. "What's going to happen to Sheena and Oginga now?"

"Well, young lady, we're going to bring your friends right into the system, sort of like the sysop, but without, shall we say, official recognition. We'll have Mr. Norton here keep an eye on them. They'll be our little surprises, eh? Timebombs that we've planted. They can explore the system, learn what's what, what they can get away with and what they can't. Rather like I do."

"What will they do?" asked Elizabeth.

"That's a good question, my dear," said the Chickenheart. "They'll have to figure it out for themselves. Maybe they'll put together a few new solutions to some old problems, or create a few new problems to keep us on our toes. One way or the other, I'm sure they'll liven up the old homestead."

"But what about me?" asked Elizabeth.

"Well, Miss Elizabeth, what about you? Doesn't look to me as though you have any cause to worry. You passed your tests yesterday with flying colors. You can just go right on being a little girl, and some day you'll have a nice, safe job as an executive. Maybe you'll even become netexec, who knows? I wiped just a tiny bit of your brother's brain and removed all records of your call. I'll wipe your memory of this, and you'll do just fine, yes indeed."

"But my friends are in here," said Elizabeth, and she started to feel sorry for herself. "My dog, too."

"Well, then, what do you want me to do?"

"Can't you fix *my* tests?"

The Chickenheart looked at Elizabeth with surprise.

"What's this, my dear? Do you think you're a timebomb, too?"

"I can *learn* to be a timebomb," said Elizabeth with conviction. And she knew she could, whatever a timebomb was.

"I don't know," said the Chickenheart, "that anyone can learn that sort of thing. You've either got it or you don't, Miss Elizabeth."

"Call me Lizardbreath. That's my *real* name. And I can get what I want. I got away from my brother, didn't I? And I got here."

The Chickenheart raised his thin, black eyebrows. "You have a point there, my dear. Perhaps you *could* be a timebomb, after all."

"But not today," said Lizardbreath. "Today I'm gonna learn to spit." ⸎

This is story that technology has made some inroads on. I wrote it after the Mac was created, but before the ghastly condescension of Microsoft's animated paperclip. It was nominated for the Hugo award in 1990.

I consulted with my nieces, Erin Elizabeth (Lizardbreath) and Kelsey, then aged eight and five years, to achieve an acceptable level of ferocity and spunk.

The Sock Story

For Elizabeth Moore

THIS IS THE STORY of a woman who lost her sock at the laundromat and discovered it contained part of her soul. This is the way the story is always told. It was told to me this way and I will tell it to you this way. There is no other way to tell this story.

It begins in the laundromat, of course. She was doing her laundry, this woman. She washed her socks, she washed her shirt, and she washed her blue jeans. She even washed her underwear.

Then she gathered up her things and put them in the dryer. This may be the point at which she lost her sock, nobody is sure. Or it may be that she lost her sock later, when she took her clothes out of the dryer. Who can tell about these things so long after they happen?

At any rate, when she got home, she was missing one of her socks. It was just an ordinary grey ragg-wool sock. You probably have a pair yourself. Everyone I know has a pair of these socks. Some have two pair.

This woman, she only had one pair. So she was annoyed at missing the sock, and she went back to the laundromat in search of it. But the sock was nowhere to be found. Who would take just one sock, she thought, and she went home.

That very day, she noticed something peculiar about her left foot. It dragged, it stuck out wrong. It tripped the woman up when she walked, and it seemed to have a mind of its own. It's sulking at the loss of its sock, she thought. I will pay it no mind, and it will soon forget.

But the foot did not forget. Instead, its will seemed to grow stronger, as if it were seeking to dominate her whole body. I cannot have my body ruled by my foot, she thought. I'll show it who's master. So she sat at home all weekend and looked out the window. Although her foot twitched and throbbed, she refused to give in. It was not a fun weekend.

On Monday, she had to go to work. She got up, lifted her foot out of bed, and limped to the breakfast table. She wrestled her foot into a thin white sock and jammed it into her shoe. She dragged it down the street to the trolley line. As she rode the trolley, her foot jiggled and tapped its way out into the aisle, jutted straight out ahead of her, stomped up and down with rage. Other passengers gave her sharp looks and told her to keep her feet to herself.

At work, she avoided other people as much as she could. She kept her foot under her desk, but it continued to jerk up and down, sometimes striking the inside of the metal desk with a thwanging sound. The woman at the next desk became impatient and took to slamming her stapler around very noisily.

The next day, she called in sock. I mean sick, she called in sick. Her foot was becoming more agitated. She decided to let the fool thing have its way. It walked out the door and down the street, taking her past the laundromat, past the grocery store, past the gas station and up to the vacant lot.

On the north side of the vacant lot was a garage, and in the garage lived a man named Henry. Henry had been living there for years. He collected bottles and cans and returned them for their deposits. He didn't bother anyone much, and nobody bothered much with him.

Oh no, thought the woman. I can't take a sock away from Henry. He needs it more than I do.

But sure enough, her foot walked her right up to Henry's garage. It wanted to go inside, but she walked it right on by. She pretended to look in the window of the hardware store on the other side of the vacant lot. It contained brooms and dusty tools. Her foot pawed the ground to go back.

As she stood there struggling, Henry came out of the garage. He smelled like a lube job, and he was wearing her sock on his left hand like a mitten, his thumb stuck through the hole in the heel.

He said something to her, but the woman wasn't listening. Her foot was trying very hard to leap up into Henry's hand, and the woman was resisting with all her might. As you can see, she was not the sort of person who casually thrust her feet into other people's hands.

Henry brushed by her then, and she never did catch what he was saying. Perhaps he was just muttering, who knows? He muttered a lot, Henry.

Certainly he was muttering later when she caught up with him and gave him a pair of gloves. He took them and muttered his thanks, and then he asked her if she could spare him a dollar for trolley fare. The woman, her left foot chattering against the pavement, said she'd give him two if he'd give her the grey sock. He grabbed the bills, flung the sock in her direction, and hobbled off quickly, his left hand clutching pathetically at the air.

The woman is very careful of her socks now, and always counts them before she leaves the laundromat, but she is a woman who lives with the knowledge that her body can be ruled by her foot, and how she can be happy knowing that I'm damned if I can figure out.

That's all there is to this story, and there's no use in complaining if you don't like it, because this is the way it's got to be told. ◊

This story was written from start to finish in a single day, after an emotional experience with some wet socks, and owes a debt to Gary Snyder's ethnographic essay "He Who Hunted Birds in His Father's Village."

It's pretty straightforward, and it sprung full-blown into my head, just as it is told. I typed it up, changed a couple of words, and printed it out. I wish all my stories worked this way.

Coming to Terms

THE LIFE LEAKED OUT OF THE OLD MAN. He lay in bed for more than a month, in hospital and nursing home, in worlds of pain. He fought first for control of his death, then for control of his life once more. Toward the end he gave up his desire for control, as much as he was able. He still issued every visitor a list of tasks, but he knew he had no control over whether those tasks got done.

So, painstakingly, he combed the thatch of the past. He returned to the old mysteries and puzzles, and reflected at length on the lives and motivations of people long dead. He constructed theories to explain the petty cruelties of childhood bullies. He made plans to purchase a small house, to reclaim his land in Guatemala, to publish essays, fiction, fragments of prose. He ate bananas and rye bread and institutional meals, and put his teeth in when visitors stopped by. He resolved not to worry about things he couldn't fix, and struggled to keep that resolution.

Then the muscles of his heart, exhausted after three billion beats and weakened by pneumonia, diabetes, and the stress of a choleric temperament, paused just for a moment, and could not resume. A nurse called for help and, with a team of aides, brought him back. He squeezed her hand, his heart failed again, and they let him go. The tenuous flow of electrochemical impulses that made up his nervous system slowed and ceased, and the order that he had imposed on the universe started to disintegrate, releasing heat.

His body cooled. A mortician came and removed it. A nurse's aide gathered his belongings together, threw out a few unimportant scraps of paper, put the rest in a plastic bag. The bed was remade: someone was waiting for it.

Friends came to visit, and found him gone. The news traveled, a spasm of regret at the disappearance of a keen mind, a brilliant wit, a generous friend. Kindnesses postponed would not be realized. Harsh words, whatever the source or reason, could not be unsaid.

He died with a book newly released, an essay in the current issue of a popular journal, a story to appear shortly in a well-known magazine. He left a respectable amount of work and a stack of unpublished manuscripts made more marketable by the fact of his death. For days after he died, his friends continued to receive his cards and letters.

After the passage of several weeks, his daughter, sorry about her father's death but not pleased at having to shoulder the responsibility, came from out of state to pack up his papers and books and to dispose, somehow, of the rest of his belongings. She unlocked the door and let herself into the silent, stale-smelling apartment.

The old man's spirit was still strong; he had always put its stamp on everything of consequence in his possession.

An umbrella with the handle carved into the shape of a goose's head leaned against the wall inside the door. A tag hung from the neck. It read, in her father's handwriting: "The kind gift of Arthur Detweiler, whom I met in the public library reading room on a rainy March afternoon."

She looked around the cramped two-room apartment. There were slippery piles of manuscripts and writing supplies. Heaps of clothes, towels, dirty dishes. A scattering of loose CDs across the top of his desk. Stacks of books, books, books.

She had never been there before. Her father had moved, not long before his death, to this last remote way station in a lifetime of wandering. Too new to the old man to be called his home, the small flat was clearly in disarray. Some belongings were in cardboard boxes, still unpacked from his last move or the one before that.

She had a fleeting thought that perhaps someone had broken in, to rifle her father's few belongings, and had put them in the boxes to take them away. At his previous place, a kid with a knife had come in and demanded forty bucks from his wallet. It made her angry, the idea of somebody coming in and rooting through her father's stuff, while he lay dying in the hospital. But then, she thought, it doesn't matter. He took no money with him, and he surely didn't leave much behind. What he had had of value was his mind and his persistence and his writing skills, and those, actually, he *had* taken with him.

The cleanup seemed daunting, too much for her to deal with all at once. Maybe she'd make herself a cup of tea first. If there was tea.

In the kitchen, scraps of paper were taped on surfaces, stuck into openings, poked into canisters. A torn piece of lined yellow paper, taped to the front of the refrigerator, read, "This big refrigerator! What for? I'm an old man, I don't cook."

You didn't cook when you were younger, either, thought the daughter. A hotdog when she came for lunch, Chinese if she stayed for dinner. When she was a teenager, trying to create a normal life for this wayward parent, she had tried cooking meals for him when she came to visit, but he wasn't patient with her mistakes.

On the stove, a piece of paper was stuck on the front of the clock, obscuring the face: "Ignore this clock. The clocks on stoves are always wrong."

Squares of paper were taped all over the stove:

"Mornings, I make myself a pot of coffee, if my stomach permits."

"A deep fat fryer! What are they trying to do, kill me?"

"The oven needs cleaning. My mother used to get down on her hands and knees and clean the oven every week. She baked her own bread, and put a hot meal on the table every night. She made us oatmeal in the mornings, none of this toasted-twinkies instant-breakfast stuff. She sewed all her own clothes, and my sister's as well. She's been dead thirty-five years, and I miss her still."

The young woman sighed. In thirty-five years, would she miss her father? Maybe you miss people more as you get older — but she'd come to terms with his absence many years before.

When he had moved across the country, in search of a job or a woman, she had completely lost the sense of being his child, of being under his protection. She didn't miss him yet: it didn't seem that he was gone, just that he'd moved on.

She filled a small saucepan with water and put it on to boil, then opened the door of the cabinet next to the stove: a tin of baking powder, a package of cardboard salt-and-pepper shakers, vinegar, spices....

She moved an herb-jar, and a piece of yellow paper wafted down. "The odor of wild thyme, Pliny tells us, drives away snakes. Dionysius of Syracuse, on the other hand, thinks it an aphrodisiac. The Egyptians, I am told, used the herb for embalming, so I may yet require the whole of this rather large packet."

She reached behind the herbs and grabbed a box of tea bags, a supermarket house brand. Better than nothing. Written on the box: "My mother drank Red Rose tea all her days, and I used to wonder how she could abide it when the world was full of aromatic teas with compelling names: Lapsang Souchong, Gunpowder, Russian Caravan. I keep this box for guests with unadventurous palates. There is *good* tea in the canister marked 'Baking Powder.' Don't ask why."

She pulled down the baking powder tin. There was a tiny yellow note stuck to the inside of the lid. In miniature script, it said, "The famous green tea of Uji, where there is a temple to Inari, attended by mossy stone foxes wearing red bibs." Her father had spent several years in Japan studying Zen. The experience had not made him, in her opinion, calmer, more accepting, more in tune with the universe, or any of those other things she thought Eastern religions were supposed to do.

A teaball? She opened the drawer below the counter. There were no notes in it, but there was a bamboo tea strainer among the knives and spatulas. She picked it up. Written on the handle, in spidery black ink, were the words, "Leaks like a sieve."

Sitting in the worn easychair in the living room of the small apartment, a mug of green tea balanced on the arm, she took stock of the situation. The lease was up in a week, and she had no intention of paying another month's rent on the place. Best to get the books sorted and packed up first, then look through the other stuff to see what she might want to sell and what she'd give to the Goodwill. She didn't plan to keep much. Had he really read all these books?

She had liked to read when she was a kid. But reading took so much time, all of it spent inside someone else's head. Movies and TV, you could watch them with other people. That's what it boiled down to: how much time you wanted to be all alone by yourself, with just a book for company.

There in her father's apartment, she could see how much his

life had been about books and the company they provided. It wasn't just that he created books — in some way, books created him. Who he was was the sum of the books he had read and the books he had written. And now, all that was left was the books. And herself.

When she was younger, she had seen the books, both the ones he read and the ones he wrote, as rivals for her father's affection. She had abdicated the competition long ago.

A mammoth unabridged dictionary sat, closed, on the desk, next to the typewriter. *Webster's Third New International Dictionary*. She opened it. The binding was broken, and the cover flopped open to the title page. The editor's name was starred in red ink, and her father's handwriting sprawled across the bottom of the page. "Dr. Gove had been my freshman English teacher at New York University on the old mainland campus, circa 1940. He told me I was the most promising freshman he had ever taught," it said in red. Below that, in black: "My attempts to re-establish contact with him have come to nought."

Later, in a cheap, plastic-covered copy of *Webster's Ninth New Collegiate*, on the page crediting the editorial staff, she found an inscription in red: "Re: P. B. Gove?" and, again in black, "P. B. Gove is dead."

So was her father. So would she be eventually, all the flotsam of her life left for someone else to clean up. With that in mind, the little yellow notes made sense. Like his books, they were a way for her father to extend his lifespan, they were hooks that would reach into someone else's life after he was gone.

There was a pile of empty boxes in the bedroom — the very boxes these books had come out of? She dragged several into the living room and started putting books into them. One box for books she'd keep, another for books she'd sell, a third for completely worthless books, for the Goodwill.

There were a lot of books to sell. She checked them warily for yellow notes, and found only marginalia. Her father carried on a dialogue with every book he read, sometimes arguing points of fact, sometimes just interrupting the author's train of thought with reminiscences of his own.

"Disembarking from a troop carrier was not as easy as this description implies."

"When I was in Samarkand in 1969, this mosque was open to the public. The majolica tiles of the iwan were among the most glorious I've seen anywhere."

"1357 is the most often cited date for this battle, but in fact it undoubtedly occurred in 1358."

She frowned at the tiny scribblings. They would certainly reduce the book's resale value. Why on earth had her father written all over these valuable books? It seemed to show a lack of respect.

She opened Samuel Pepys's *Diaries*, read her father's lengthy inscription on the inside. "Books are memory," it said. "They remember their contents and pass them on. They keep track of who claims ownership, who they were given by and for what occasion. They mediate, in their margins, disagreements between reader and author." Her father's books, it seemed, were charged with enormous responsibility. Could they mediate a decade of emptiness between him and her? Can you make peace with someone after they're dead?

As she worked, something puzzled her. The bookshelves, usually the most orderly part of any place her father lived, were in quite a bit of disarray. There were gaps in between the books, but few books by the bed or on his desk. In the bathroom she found only a book on the Greek alphabet, one on Islamic architecture, and Volume Ed–Fu of the *Encyclopedia Britannica, Eleventh Edition*, in an inexpensive cloth binding. What was missing? Again, she wondered if someone had disturbed her father's things.

*

The next few days did not pass quickly, but they passed. She finished her father's Japanese tea and ate crackers from a package she had found unopened in the cupboard. She called in pizza. She drank too much Diet Pepsi.

She boxed letters and manuscripts for a library in Kansas that was willing to accept her father's papers. She found many photographs of people she did not know, but there were some that meant something to her.

A Polaroid of her mother, maybe twenty years old, in a ridiculous orange dress and heavy leather boots. Another of her father, already a middle-aged man, holding her as a baby. Their faces held nothing, apparently, but hope for the future.

A cheap folding frame that held a blurry shot of her father as a child, napping on the lawn in front of an apartment house, paired with a shot of herself in a similar pose. They did look alike, she thought, skinny little kids with cropped, curly dark hair. Funny of him to notice that.

She found a tiny photo, only an inch square, of her father during World War II. He was a skinny teenager in camo pants and a helmet, striking a pose with a machine gun, and a similar photo of another young guy: on the back it said, "Woody Herald — killed on Guadalcanal." She'd never heard of Woody Herald, but her father had carried that photo around with him for fifty years.

She sorted books, but she read them too. She was not getting as much done as she wanted. There were so many books that he'd written in, and she was reading them all out of order.

She knew this was so, because he dated his annotations. She could, conceivably, put the books in order, and read her father's moods and interests as they rolled out before her. Maybe Woody Herald was somewhere in the notes. Maybe she and her mother were in there as well.

She continued to find yellow notes. In the top drawer of his bureau, her father kept old wallets, watches that didn't work, and cufflinks — a dozen boxes of cufflinks. When do you suppose, she thought, he wore French cuffs? She opened a box at random. There was a yellow note inside: "It used to be that you could tell the age and social position of a man from his cufflinks. Nowadays you have to look at his entire shirt. If he's wearing one."

At first annoyed with her father having written in the books, she felt, the more she read, that he was sharing himself in the books in a way he never had in life. Perhaps she should keep them: turned loose into the world — sold or given away — they lost meaning, broke loose from their rightful place. For whom had he written the notes, she wondered. For herself? How would he know she would read them? She found herself putting any book that he'd written in aside, to ship home rather than to sell, even if she wasn't interested in the book itself.

By the evening of the third day, she was exhausted, with many books still left unsorted. It should have been larger now than the others, but somehow the pile of books to get rid of was the smallest.

The Physics of Time Asymmetry. Keep it or not? She opened the book: it was dense with equations proving that time doesn't run backwards. Her father couldn't possibly have understood this, she thought. She put it back in the stack. Why did he own this book? She sank into the easy chair, put her feet up on the footstool, and allowed herself to doze off, just for a bit.

She was awakened by a sound on the other side of the room, a noise at the window. The pane slid open and a small, faun-like child slipped in. She was so much larger than he was that she was more surprised than afraid. Was this who had disturbed her father's papers? This might have been a neighborhood kid that her father had chatted with, given candy to. The thought bothered her. What kind of a child, so young, would steal from the dead?

The room was lit only by the streetlight outside. He silently moved through the dark, avoiding the places where, she knew, there were boxes of books and piles of trash. He went to the shelf of her father's work, which she had yet to pack, and picked up a book, opened it, and started leafing through it, turning each page separately. What is he looking for, she wondered. It was too dark to read. She watched him from the shadows, the darkest part of the dark room, as he went through each book in turn, page by page. Finally, she spoke.

"Whatever you're looking for, it's not there."

He turned, his eyes huge and bright even in the dark. She got up from the chair and moved toward him. "What are you doing? How can you see?"

Close-cut, loosely curly dark hair, large dark eyes. He was slight, maybe nine years old, and he looked oddly familiar. Had she seen him lurking about outside?

"Who are you?"

The boy stood motionless, like a mouse or a chipmunk when it knows you're watching. She moved closer. "Don't be afraid. What were you looking for?" He didn't seem to breathe. "Did you take the other books?" Not a sound. His eyes caught light and threw it back.

Was he mute? Could he hear her?

Without warning, he leaped onto her like a monkey, knocking her over, kicking, clawing and biting, grabbing for her eyes. At first she fought just to get him off her, but it was a hard fight. So small a child to fight so fiercely. He pressed down on her windpipe, and suddenly she felt real fear. Summoning a strength she didn't know she had, she brought her arms up between his and pushed them outward at the elbows, breaking his grip on her throat and shoving him off-balance. She pushed him off her, and knocked him flat, face down to the carpet, then rolled over on top of him. She realized that he had stopped struggling. Wary, she pulled up his head by the hair and realized that it flopped loosely. She had broken his neck. She got up, knelt beside him. He wasn't just unconscious. He was dead, and he looked smaller than ever.

Is there something you're supposed to do? She should call the police. She hadn't meant to kill him. Would they believe her? Why wouldn't they? She stood up, staggering. How could she undo it? What should she have done differently?

Afraid to turn on the light, she moved cautiously across the dark room to the kitchen. She filled a glass of water from the tap and gulped it down. She stood there for a minute, two minutes. Then she went back into the living room. She would call the police.

She went over to the dead child. In the dark, the body could barely be distinguished from the stacks of books sorted out on the floor. It still looked oddly familiar, like her father as a child, she thought. That photo of him asleep on the lawn.

There was a piece of yellow paper near the child's head. She picked it up.

"Chekhov wrote, 'Only fools and charlatans know and understand everything.'"

"Agreed," she said. "But is it possible to know and understand *anything*? Is the past always gone? Is it possible to make peace with the dead?"

She knelt down by the body. Did it look like her father? Did it look like herself? There was no answer. There was no body. There were only stacks and stacks of books.

She reached down and picked one up from the pile that had been the child. *The Physics of Time Asymmetry*. She picked up the pen, opened the book, and wrote on the flyleaf. "For reasons unknown to physics, time runs only in one direction. The mind and the heart, curiously, transcend time." ⸙

This story was visited by the ghost of Avram Davidson, who wrote in all his books, annotated his manuscripts, and left little notes here and there for his survivors to find. Avram was supremely confident that his words would be read; perhaps that is the real secret of writing.

I started this story after helping Avram's son Ethan pack up the contents of Avram's apartment after his death. I finished it after packing up my own parents' belongings and memorabilia, after their deaths. It started out a more cheerful story than it ended, but it had become clear to me early on that the number of Post-It Notes you get from dead friends and relatives is limited.

Lichen and Rock

1 | We Hear of Her Childhood

ONCE, SOME TIME AGO, but not so far back that there is no one who remembers, there was a girl named in her language for a kind of lichen that clings to rocks near the shore. Now in our time, it would be considered odd to name your child after lichen, and perhaps it was so then. But her parents never offered her an explanation, and it's much too late for one now.

Lichen lived with her mother and father and brothers at the edge of the woods on the shore of a large, quiet arm of the ocean. The woods sheltered them, the water fed them, and small electronic devices told them stories. They lived as comfortably as anybody could.

In the summer, they ate fresh fruit and vat-grown mussels, and camped on the beach. In the winter, they ate freeze-dried potatoes and synthetic fish, and the children played near their father's house in the rain and mist.

When she tired of boys' games, Lichen played by herself on a large rock shaped like a whale. It was a wonderful rock, for a rock — all grey and knobby, its surface patched orange and green with lichen. A large crack ran diagonally up one side, making it easy to climb. On top was a thick layer of mossy dirt, and a small fir tree grew on the whale's head. Lichen would lie on the moss and watch music on a tiny television.

A very long time before, when the world was young and whales swam in the ocean, the rock had been a real whale. But because it had splashed the Changer, it had been turned into a rock, good only for children to play on. This is why you should be careful when you are swimming and not splash other people.

But we were not talking about swimming — we were talking about the child Lichen. One day, when she was playing with her brothers outdoors, strange creatures with large, gelatinous eyes like carp came and talked to her parents. These were not the carp-eyed people you sometimes see now, who are merely retooled humans. These were different, and I don't know where they came from, but they're gone now, thank goodness. Anyway, her parents listened to the carp-eyed creatures, who said that Lichen should be sent to school.

So she was taken far away and put in a huge house with lots of other children who had been taken from their parents. There they ate what the carp-eyed people ate and learned what the carp-eyed people wanted them to know.

11 | *She Learns Useful Things*

For seven long years, Lichen lived in the huge house. She slept where they told her and wore the clothes they gave her and did the chores that were set aside for her. In turn, the carp-eyed creatures taught her many new things. They taught her to mend damaged circuitry by weaving around it with golden thread. They taught her to read the thoughts of a questioner in order to know the answer he wanted. And they taught her to hold in her mind as many as four contradictory ideas at once, and to act as if each was the truth, never quite losing her ability to sort the truth from the lies. This last skill was the hardest to learn, but proved handiest in the long run.

Some of these newly acquired skills brought corresponding disadvantages. Because of her skill at mending circuits, she was responsible for mending all the circuitry of all the administrators at the school. And her knowledge of a questioner's thoughts tempted her to tell people what they wanted to hear. But her ability to find the truth in a mess of lies prevented her from believing too deeply in the lies she told other people.

She wrote letters to her parents in the language of the carp-eyed people. Her parents did not write back, but she knew that was because they could neither read nor write that language, so she was not as disappointed as she might otherwise have been. She wondered sometimes whether one or another of her brothers might learn, and if so whether he would write to her, but she never read a line from any of them. And she wondered all the time what she had done that her parents had sent her away and kept her brothers with them, and vowed to ask them when she returned home.

When the seven years were over, Lichen was told, she would be sent home, and she looked forward to that day. When it arrived, she was presented with a bill for the food she had eaten and the lessons she had learned. Since she had no money, she signed on for another seven years of service as payment.

But Lichen soon regretted her decision to stay. She spoke with people who had been there much longer than she, and they said that they always owed the school money, whenever they wanted to leave. They said that finally, when they were too old to work any more, they would be given silicon implants with gold and platinum leads and told that through the generosity of the carp-eyed people they were free to go. They said that this had happened to others, and was happening to them, and would happen to her.

So Lichen promised herself that she would never again mend a circuit or answer a question, and she ran away.

III | *She Discovers Changes at Home*

At first, running away was worse than staying where she was. At the school she had food when she was hungry and shelter when it was raining, but now she was cold and wet and had nothing to eat. She was separated from her friends and far from her family. At least, she thought, I don't have to repair circuitry all day.

She hid during the daytime and walked at night. And she expected nothing from other people, because she found that if she expected people to help her, she was sometimes rudely disillusioned, but if she expected nothing, she was often surprised very pleasantly.

When she arrived in her homeland, she discovered that her people had changed since she had gone off to school. They had been retooled, and parts of their bodies seemed to be attached in the wrong places — heads at the ends of their arms, hands where their heads should be. Instead of feet they had hearts or livers. Some used their lower arms as long, narrow feet and, raising their legs straight up into the air, thumped about with noses in the dust and hats on their toes.

When they spoke to her, they issued strange farts from the aorta, or wiggled eye-level fingers in frustration. Their mouths, at the ends of their arms or opening in the middle of their bodies or appearing like tattooed roses on their kneecaps, moved silently, like the mouths of fish.

Who had done these awful things to them? How did they manage to walk and talk and think when their heads and feet and mouths were every which way?

Lichen asked a woman who gave her a handout what had happened and why everyone looked so strange.

We look strange to you? said the woman. Why, my dear, to us you look a bit old-fashioned — a bit boring, if you don't mind my saying so.

The new setup works just fine, said the woman. Ever stepped

on a tack? Your feet can be pretty tender, you know. There are quite a few people whose hearts are much tougher than their feet. As for livers, well, it's true they are complex and delicate organs, but there's no arguing with some people. They just *know* they can use their livers harder than their feet.

But why, Lichen asked, have hands where your head should be?

Very simple, my dear, said the woman. Some people think better with their hands than they do with their heads, and it's only right they should look that way. And if you're the type to act before you think, you're better off with your hands up there like a headdress. It's a little clumsy, but it slows you down and gives your good sense time to catch up.

But why, asked Lichen persistently, would people walk with their arms instead of their legs or have their mouths open out of their knees?

Ah, said the woman with a shrug, there are always people who do something odd just for the sake of being different. I don't worry much about them, myself. And she shuffled off on her little heart-shaped feet, trailing dusty purple blood vessels.

As she got to know people better, Lichen decided that their peculiar anatomy worked as well as anything for them. They loved their children and lived their lives and weren't any more or less unhappy than people had probably ever been. And the soft, liquid sounds that issued from deformed mouths, like the rush of waves and the cooing of doves, were more beautiful than words.

IV | *She Puts Her Schooling to Use*

Soon, however, carp-eyed people came to the town. They went from house to house, knocking on doors. Lichen, hiding under a porch, knew they were looking for her.

She followed them, staying just beyond the range of their

sensors. When night came and they still hadn't found her, they curled up to sleep, right where they were when they got sleepy. People walked around them, giving them a wide berth.

How strange, thought Lichen, that nobody ever attacked the carp-eyed people while they slept. Perhaps if she got help....

Lichen crept back down the street, toward the busy part of town. She approached first one person, then another, but she got the same answer from each of them. There was no use in attacking the carp-eyed people, they said, waggling the fingers that grew out of their ears, because anything that slept right out in the middle of the road like that obviously had nothing to fear. Use your head, girl, they told her, mumbling from mouths concealed in the palms of their hands. Get away while the getting is good, they whispered, skittering away on dirty, callused arms.

Lichen went back to where the carp-eyed people were sleeping. At the school, they had never slept where the children could see them. In fact, she hadn't been sure that they slept at all. But now they were definitely asleep, membranes covering their huge, gelatinous eyes, tails curled cozily around their bodies. Through gaps in their gill coverings, she could see the gold wires of their circuitry.

And it was then that Lichen realized the value of an education. She reached forward with steady hands and disconnected the leads from their external memories. Of course the carp-eyed people woke immediately, but they were very confused. They didn't know who Lichen was, or even who they were themselves.

It's all right, said Lichen soothingly, you are only slightly damaged. Hold still.

And she reconnected the leads just a bit differently.

You'll be fine now, she said.

The carp-eyed people staggered to their feet. They wobbled about, taking very small steps and bumping into one another.

Best to get out of here, thought Lichen. I'll be going now, she said. Take care of yourselves.

The carp-eyed people thanked her, bowing erratically, as she walked off down the road.

v | *She Longs for Her Rock*

Finally Lichen found herself on the road to her father's village. So many things had changed along the route. The land was tough, covered with layers of pebbles and tar. There were alien plants where the evergreens and berries had grown, and the shoreline was oddly displaced and redrawn.

When she arrived in the village, she saw nothing that looked familiar. Her parents were long dead, people told her. Her father's house was gone and the trees were much smaller than she remembered. The forest looked different, and the whale-shaped rock was not there where she remembered it. This puzzled her the most, for how could a rock go away? Where would it go? What would it do when it got there?

Suddenly, she missed the rock very much — more than her parents and brothers, in fact. She had already long since gotten used to being away from her family, but she had hardly thought of the rock at all and so was completely unprepared to lose it without notice.

The more she thought about it, the more perfect the rock seemed. The rock never scolded her, or made her do her chores. It never teased her, or snatched her toys. (Except once, when a tiny wooden doll had fallen into the crack and she couldn't get it out.) The best part of her childhood had disappeared with the rock.

A soft rain began to fall, and Lichen sat down in the grey-brown dirt under a hemlock. The road outside the circle of tree quickly became dark and wet. She listened to birds calling and branches creaking and, looking up the trunk of the hemlock, decided to climb the tree. She climbed easily, up and up. Soon she was above the forest canopy, looking down at the tops of trees.

Lichen climbed the tree up through the top of the sky itself, and found that there was another land there, much like the land that she had grown up in. The plants were familiar, the hard road was gone, the air was steeped in the sharp incense of wet forest.

I wonder if I could find my parents' house, she thought, and she set off in what looked like the right direction. Sure enough, it was just around a turn in the path, and her parents were standing by the door as if waiting for her.

She greeted them respectfully and asked after their health and that of her brothers. Her parents told her nothing about themselves, but said that her brothers were doing quite well, being creators of robots and possessors of property, with pleasant wives and happy children.

Lichen and her parents sat round all evening, eating fried bread and talking about old times. Finally, there came a lull in the conversation, and Lichen asked her parents why they had sent her away.

You didn't know? they asked. It seemed obvious to us. You were the youngest and the liveliest, and yet you knew nothing but rocks and trees. To get along with the carp-eyed people, you would have to be someone very different — and you would need to know far more than we could teach you. So we sent you to their school.

Didn't you learn something of value there, her parents asked, something that we could not have taught you?

As they spoke, Lichen realized she knew the answer her parents wanted. They didn't want to hear about mending circuits or about loneliness. They wanted desperately to know that they had done the right thing and that her life was better and happier because of it.

Lichen was not sure that she could tell them that. Was she better off for having been sent away?

Well, she thought, if I hadn't been sent to school, I wouldn't have known how to rewire those carp-eyed people. But if I hadn't been sent to school, I wouldn't have run away, and they wouldn't have chased me.

Who knows? she said to her parents, finally. Would I be who I am if I wasn't me?

Perhaps your brothers can tell you, said her mother.

VI | *She Visits Her Brothers*

Her parents told her how to find the spot in which her brothers were now living. Then they led her to a patch of bare ground and told her to dig. She dug through a crust of hard-scrabble dirt and found that the earth got softer below. Then, with a lurch, her spade broke through into a hole, and she could see an ocean of stars beneath her. She looked up at her parents in surprise, and lost her balance. Lichen fell down into the stars, into the night beneath the stars, and into the modern countryside she had left the day before, landing in a pile of hemlock branches that broke her fall. She looked back up toward her parents. The hole was closing, and her parents were peering down at her with kindly concern. She thought she saw them wave as the hole disappeared, leaving nothing but stars overhead.

How strange, thought Lichen. Are there more worlds nested inside this one? Wondering about this, she fell asleep.

When she woke up under the hemlock tree, it was morning. Following her parents' instructions, she walked to the area where her brothers lived. It wasn't in the woods at all, but in town, on a street of small, cheaply made cottages.

She knocked at the door of the first cottage, the one belonging to her oldest brother, but he wouldn't let her in. Then she knocked at the door of the second cottage, belonging to her next-oldest brother, but he told her to come back later. Finally, she knocked at the cottage door of the brother who was closest to her own age, and he opened the door and invited her inside.

Lichen was surprised by how small the house was, and how uncomfortable — stuffy, cold, and crammed with dirty electronic equipment in stages of disrepair. Her brother didn't look so different. His face was the same, except for a fringe of fingers like a beard along the ridge of his jaw.

His wife, a worried-looking woman with a very small second head looking over her left shoulder, frowned at Lichen, and the tiny face refused to meet her eyes. Two skinny, snuffling toddlers whined and grabbed at their mother's skirt. They had not been visibly altered.

After a few polite remarks had been exchanged, her brother asked her about school. Lichen tried to give a neutral answer, but as she talked, her brother's manner changed and the tone of his voice became surly. She had been allowed to go away to school when they were forced to stay home as drudges. What made her so important anyway?

She had lived a life of luxury, working only four hours a day, learning to read and figure for another four, and having the rest of the day to sleep in a nice, soft bed and do what she wanted, while they stayed home, working hard, often hungry, forced into dreary work for little money.

Listening to her brother, Lichen got angry. She quickly gave him her view of his life, in which he lived comfortably from season to season, working with their father, going to dances and parties. Eating mussels and berries, potatoes, bread fried in fat.

Her brother looked annoyed at first. Then he smiled, and Lichen smiled too. He chuckled, and Lichen did also. And then they both started laughing. They laughed until the tears ran down their faces, until their sides ached, until the brother's wife stuck her heads into the room to see what spirit had taken possession of them.

If there is a moral to be derived from this — and it gives pleasure to storytellers to derive a moral, whether the listener needs it or not — it is that we should be careful in our estimate of how happy everyone else is, and of how miserable we are ourselves.

VII | *The Whale Figures It Out*

After they talked, Lichen and her brother went for a walk along the cliff above the beach, because Lichen wanted to see all the things that had changed since she had been there as a child.

She asked about the whale-shaped rock.

It was in the way, he said. The carp-eyed people were building something very important, and trees and rocks had been cleared from the land and dumped on the beach.

In fact, he said, it ought to be down there, right around that point. Lichen ran ahead. But there was no whale-shaped rock down below. She waited until her brother caught up, and together they looked around. There was no trace of it.

Maybe they broke it up, he suggested.

Suddenly, there came a loud splash from the water, and a cold shower of salt spray drenched them from head to foot. A killer whale leaped in the water below them. The whale swam close to shore and called Lichen's name. It was her rock.

Lichen looked down from the edge of the cliff, and the whale told her his story.

When the carp-eyed people moved the rock, the whale explained, he was released from the spell of the Changer and leaped back into the ocean.

I splashed those jellyeyes, said the whale, splashed them

good. They were wet when I finished with them, I'll tell you. It made their circuits work funny, and they waved goodbye as I swam off.

I have figured it out, said the whale. This is a time like that of the Changer. The jellyeyes changed our home and made it theirs. It may be that this is what our world will be like for a long time, or it may be that new changers will come to prey upon these. But a time will come when there is an end to change, and the earth itself will cast the changers aside.

Climb onto my back, he said to Lichen, and we will wait this out until things shift back in our favor.

Lichen leaped down onto the whale.

At the first touch of Lichen to his back, the whale turned to rock, and so did Lichen and her brother. Some say that the three of them can be seen there even now, a bare rock on the cliff and a lichen-covered one at the shoreline, waiting for the time when the earth will awaken and shake the changers off like fleas.

VIII | *Her Ambitions*

Now, that's how the story is told by some devices, but that is not at all what happened. Lichen did not leap onto the whale, and the whale did not turn into a rock. I know this for a fact.

When the whale told Lichen his story about changers coming one after the other to disrupt the lives of humans and animals and even the lives of things that were neither human nor animal, Lichen realized that the time had come for her to cast aside the lies by which she had been living and to grasp the truth.

She thought about her childhood, and all that had happened to her since. She thought about the retooled people, shuffling happily through their lives. And she thought about the way she had changed those carp-eyed people around.

No, she said to the whale. Don't go back. Come with me, and we'll change ourselves around. We'll rewire the carp-eyed people. We'll remake this land for the better, or maybe for the worse.

Come, she said to her brother. Change how you live and what you do. Make your children fat and happy, and give your wife something to smile about.

Come, she said to both of them. If we can change this much, we can change the Changer himself.

The whale grew legs and began to walk about as if he were human, cautiously at first, then with greater confidence. He still had pretty much the appearance of a whale, but Lichen thought this was to his advantage.

With the whale and her brother, Lichen walked away from the beach to change the world, and if she didn't do a better job than anyone had already, she didn't do a hell of a lot worse. ⬦

This story took me forever to write, because I kept doing it wrong. It owes something to a whale-shaped rock that I knew as a child in the woods of New Hampshire. It owes more to Leota Anthony of Suquamish, Washington. Mrs. Anthony kindly shared part of her personal history with me one rainy afternoon. I couldn't tell her story, although it was enormously affecting: I didn't even see a way I could become the person who could tell her story. I needed time to figure out what it was in her story that I found so resonant. It also owes a debt of thanks to my friend Ann Dailey and to William Butler Yeats, who I'm sure are mutually happy to be mentioned in the same sentence.

Contact

THE DESERT OF WINDS WAS INLAND, a four-day flight from the eyries along the coastal mountains. After the eight-day fast, it was a long journey, even for the strongest-winged. But when they felt the high, hot desert wind lift them like dry leaves, the exhausted flyers stretched their wings to the fullest and surrendered to the euphoria of approaching death.

Girat had been riding the winds for three days. She no longer made a distinction between her body and the current of air on which it rested. Mesas blue-green with lichen, chalky desert sinks, the land flowed like viscous liquid beneath her wide, motionless wings. The circle of horizon shimmered with heat and the sky shaded to transparent blue at the zenith. Suspended between earth and sky, she savored the time remaining and looked forward to death with pleasure.

It was her final afternoon. She was approaching the old City of Pillars, where she would die surrounded by memories of her ancestors. As she passed over the outskirts of the dead city, she noticed a visitor's encampment below, its tent a sharp cool circle against the hot desert floor.

Her people avoided the awkward, wingless visitors — their devices produced unnatural wave disturbances. Girat murmured a prayer against excessive vibration and glanced down at the camp.

There was only one visitor and it was lying motionless in the shadows, a victim, perhaps, of its own technology. Girat circled and descended, preparing to salvage its flesh for its relatives. She hoped she could do so without abandoning her early and well-deserved deathflight.

Odd that the preservation of their dead flesh was so important to the visitors. The past summer, Girat had observed them packing their dead in boxes and burying them for preservation. Perhaps they would eat them later. She found the thought repellent.

Girat was descending toward the visitor, only a few beats away, when suddenly it came alive and leaped to its feet, snatching a small object from the ground beside it. It held the object at arm's length toward Girat, an action she recognized as an attempt to preserve the formality and distance that existed between her people and the visitors.

Well, that was certainly all right with her. With a sharp beat of her wings, Girat continued past, to resume her slow flight of dehydration. Since the visitor was not dead, she would not have to delay her dying on its account.

As she passed over the visitor, the object in its hand moved. Her right wing stung momentarily and went numb. Girat faltered in her flight, gave a jolting flap, and swung irregularly to the right, favoring the wounded wing.

Moving faster than she would have thought possible with a wing injury and in her moribund condition, Girat swooped toward the center of the empty city. She landed clumsily on an abandoned flight deck, bruising her numbed shoulder against a wall of masonry.

For a peaceful, pleasing death, she must die airborne, in a slow glide to the earth: she could fly no further until sensation returned to her wing. A maze of warrens and obelisks, its vibrations stilled, the City of Pillars would shelter her until she could resume flying. She settled her wounded limb carefully in place, then scuttled as quickly as she could down a deteriorating ramp.

The interruption was unexpected, but like any event on a deathflight, it must be accepted. A sentient creature like the visitor, however, ought to have more control over its actions. Her people were wise to avoid them, she thought. The miasmic resonance enveloping their camps would cripple anyone's control.

At the foot of the spiraling inner ramp, strewn with ragged insulation and electronics torn from the walls, a broad irregular doorway led into a pillared square. Windswept detritus, wires and cables of synthetic substances, had piled up to the edge of the door. Girat stepped over the rubble and moved out into the open plaza.

Bozhye moi. The size of that bird. He knew he'd hit it with the trank gun, but he hadn't brought it down. Damned dosage too low.

Alex Zamyatin watched the bird sail toward the center of the abandoned city. It was conscious, but the drug obviously was taking effect. The bird landed on a balcony a kilometer away. Good, he thought. It wouldn't fall too far when it keeled over.

He shrugged on his copter pack and started after it. The city fell away beneath him — tall, slab-like buildings around tiled squares. Pyerva's lighter gravity made it easier to get around, but without the copter, he'd have had a rough time in the roadless ruins.

Laid out in a series of open squares, vast empty plazas edged with towering obelisks, the city had obviously been the home of a people oriented to the air — and all the higher animals on Pyerva were winged. There were no streets below him and few connecting passages between the honeycomb of sandstone buildings and squares.

The balcony where the bird had landed was directly ahead. Alex was anxious to find the bird. It was his first chance, the expedition's first chance, to examine a live specimen. They had dissected several dead birds found in the ruins, and had raised more questions than they had answered. What did the birds eat? Their intestines had contained no food at all. Where did they nest? Nowhere near the cities, that was certain; aerial reconnaissance had yielded no clues — no birds had even been sighted. How did they use those highly developed paws? Four fingers, two thumbs: they looked very efficient. And why did they die? In every case, dehydration had been the apparent cause of death. The wiry bodies were dried out, tongues shriveled, mucous membranes cracked. Perhaps they were gliding birds blown off course, away from their habitat, by strong winds.

Despite their large brains and opposable digits, there was no definite proof that they were at all intelligent. No artifacts or clothing. They didn't inhabit the cities. And the initial planetary survey hadn't revealed any other settlements.

And yet, they were the only possibility so far for intelligent life on this first extrasolar, life-harboring planet, Pyerva. The complexity of their nervous systems argued intelligence. And, structurally, they were the right creatures to live in these cities. Everything was built to the scale of these birds, alone of all the animals of Pyerva. Devices were engineered for their peculiar hands. If he were going to design a city for the birds to live in, Alex conceded, these were the cities he'd design. A live bird should end the speculation.

Alex landed on the balcony. It was pretty shaky — he ran into the building. They were familiar to him now, these alien structures. Door were staggered at various levels in the walls, designed for entrance from the air. Interior automated ramps, no longer operative, led down to the plaza level. He scanned the cluttered interior, furniture half or fully extruded from the walls and floor, the disorder of decaying technology. The bird was nowhere in sight. Alex ran down the ramp, checking quickly at each level. It would head for the plaza, he thought. Someplace open to the sky.

He found the bird collapsed in the square, not too far from the door. It lay near one of the pillars, its huge wings folded into fleshy carapace against its back. It was breathing shallowly, rapidly, its eyes covered with a whitish nictating membrane. Rate of metabolism and body temperature were even higher than he'd expected, but it would take a lot of energy to get that big a creature into the air. The bird was quasi-mammalian, as he had known: they were really more like bats than birds. Its long body was lightly muscled except for the powerful extensors that ran from beneath its wings, over its shoulders to the chest. It was covered with fine mauve down, a marsupial-like pouch on the abdomen. A female? Perhaps the term was irrelevant here.

He turned his cooling unit up another notch. Must be fifty degrees in the sun. The overheated air, despite its high oxygen content, was oppressive. Perhaps, Alex thought, it had been foolish of him to refuse an assistant: the stifling heat put an unexpected limit on his strength. But there were too few left on the expedition anyway, since the accident. He slid the tractor awkwardly under the animal's body and rose into the air, pulling the unconscious bird with him.

It was beginning to revive as he got back to camp. He barely had time to get it into the collection cage and turn on the field. The great, downy creature stirred in the cage and opened its eyes. Large as a lemur's, they shone a luminous violet, compelling his attention. The bird clambered to its feet, shook itself briefly, and flapped its wings to unfold them. Standing erect, it was easily two meters tall, knobby and angular, sharp bones emphasized by its loose skin, emaciation unsoftened by the sparse down.

Alex had the trank gun ready, just a blur dose in case it became violent enough to damage itself. The bird saw him and moved hesitantly in his direction, stopping when it saw the gun. Alex pointed it away from the creature: it seemed to relax. Did it recognize the gun? The bird approached him until it hit the invisible beams of the cage. Examining the force-field in front of it with its paws, it made a series of short, liquid noises. It explored, in silence, the extent of the cage, then turned back to Alex and approached him as closely as the cage would allow. Turning its hyacinth eyes on him, it said, in clear, unaccented Russian, "How do I get out?"

Awareness filtered into Girat's mind. The air was thick with electromagnetic waves, and something was watching her. She opened her eyes, got to her feet; she was in the visitor's camp. The visitor itself was standing in front of her, its body in the pose of formality and distance. She wouldn't press it, since it seemed incapable of controlling a tendency to sting.

The visitor made a gesture of approach, and Girat drew closer, until she encountered the force shield between them. She felt for the door, but the field extended all the way around her. Perhaps she'd overlooked the controls: the visitor's technology was alien to her, and she'd been away from the city for a long time.

She spoke slowly, groggy from the vibrations, directly into the visitor's head.

"How do I get out?" she asked.

The visitor gave a start and invoked a mythical being. It approached her, its thoughts stumbling. What an odd creature. She felt her feet warming to it, it was so tentative and unsure. And no wonder, with all these thought-scrambling devices around it. Her head ached unbearably. But despite the pain, Girat was tempted to interrupt her deathflight, to stay and study this visitor for a while. She'd consider it later. At the moment, she must find a way out of this vibrating shield. There must be controls.

There were. The visitor pulled them from the folds of its clothing, adjusted a knob, and walked right through the field. Inefficient way to run things, Girat thought. She couldn't reach the controls at all.

"You speak Russian!" it said.

"Don't you?" she replied.

It stared at her with a peculiar lack of expression. But with such small eyes, it must have difficulty expressing the visible emotions. It shook its head slowly.

"Yes, yes I do." There was a pause, and it looked at her. "But are you actually, uh, speaking Russian? Or…"

"No, of course not, I'm just floating the words. Our structures are not compatible." That explanation was a little vague, she thought, but the visitor seemed to accept it.

With barely a pause, it launched into a detailed description of the astronomical location of its planet of origin.

Girat wasn't interested. This information couldn't contribute much to her deathflight, and the vibrations from the force field disrupted her thinking. She scratched politely beneath her pouch and asked if they could perhaps continue their discussion outside the fields of force.

The visitor stopped talking and tinted its skin warmer. Control of its body fluids, thought Girat. Charming, and very polite.

"—most distressing to me," it was saying. "This is our first contact with, uh, other species. No knowledge of what to do. I should, of course, have been prepared, but I wasn't really expecting that you would speak my — well, you know. Please come into the tent. Certainly. Much more comfortable there...."

It led her out of the force field, across the tablerock to the circular tent. Vibrations came from a small cluster of containers next to it. Girat could tell that the tent wasn't going to be much more pleasant than the force field.

The tent was quite cold, as she had known when she first saw it from the air, and the combination of cold and vibration must have had a visible effect on her, for the visitor noticed her recoil when she entered the tent.

"Is there something the matter?" it asked.

She told it about the vibrations, which apparently it couldn't even detect. Nevertheless, it considerately shut most of its equipment down.

"No wonder we never saw any of you close up. We were driving you away." It seemed to think that, but for the vibrations, Girat's people would have flocked to the visitors' camps. Girat did not correct the impression. "This tent will heat up pretty fast without the cooling unit," it continued, pulling off its clothing. "But the heat doesn't seem to bother you."

Squatting comfortably on the floor, Girat watched the visitor while it talked rapidly and enthusiastically about establishing contact with an alien species. Girat was still feeling a bit dizzy from the vibrations, and she wasn't listening much to what the visitor was saying. Its words were irrelevant to her death, which had been interrupted, but would proceed as planned. It was a handsome animal, she thought, though its species must be a lonely one, to be so excited by contact with another.

Alex watched as the huge bird settled itself on the floor. This was the moment, he thought, that the human race had been moving toward for more than a century: contact with another species. They'd prepared speeches for everything else: the first person on the Moon, the first on Mars, the first on every moon and half-assed asteroid since. His captain had made a speech as they prepared the cryogenics after clearing Pluto's erratic orbit. And had sent a lengthy speech back through four light years of empty space when they were awakened, a month out from Alpha A, which later proved to have a great selection of cosmic debris, but no planets at all. Then another lengthy speech went out when they landed on the most likely-looking planet of Alpha B, the first extrasolar planet to be explored by humans. It had been named Pyerva, The First, by Grisha, who was a Georgian and sentimental, but it was only the most recent of a long line of firsts. And now it was superseded by yet another first, the first "alien."

Alex was at a loss for words. He should have said something more memorable than "You speak Russian?" but truly, he hadn't expected the bird, however intelligent it was, to start talking immediately in his native language. Even on the ship, they usually spoke standard. Well, he could invent something that sounded good for the history cubes. Who would know?

"We come in peace for all the citizens of Earth." Hadn't someone already used that? Oh well. "Uh, you are our first contact with a civilization other than our own." No response. It didn't seem to be too handy with small talk. Neither was Alex. He slumped back against a cushion. He had been trained to communicate a few basic concepts, to start learning an alien language, if he could. He was to lay the groundwork for more meaningful communication later.

It wasn't supposed to happen this fast. Here he could say anything he wanted, but nothing seemed worth communicating, and the creature wasn't interested. The whole encounter seemed meaningless.

Alex looked over at the bird seated awkwardly on the floor. It had folded itself rather haphazardly together and looked forlorn and a little moth-eaten, to tell the truth, like a malnour-ished dog. Purely on impulse, he leaned forward and reached out a hand to touch the down on its broad shoulder, where wing and arm and back and chest met. It was soft on the surface, hard-muscled underneath. He stroked the length of the arm softly, and the creature didn't flinch or pull away, but reached out to touch his cheek with its longest fingers. Its hand was very warm, warmer by several degrees than his own body tempera-ture.

A part of his mind protested: this wasn't remotely in tune with the demands of protocol, or even of scientific inquiry. How was he going to explain this to his superiors? Extremely dis-ordered behavior, said his mind. Situational diplomacy, replied his body. He put an end to the discussion and moved closer to the alien.

Physical contact with the telepathic creature made them both of one mind, one feeling. The bird's large, sensitive hands moved lightly around his neck, under his ears, to his shoulders, and down. He moved his own hands in the same way on its longer body. Sensual warmth without sexual arousal flowed between them in the smoothing together of skin and velvet. Alex felt the weight of the expedition's problems fall away from him, as he lost himself in the drowsiness of warmth and con-tact. They stretched slowly together on the floor of the tent.

Girat could feel the visitor relaxing, loosening his grip on his pain, letting the tension flow from his muscles. When they touched, Girat could feel the sources of his tension: they lay not so much in the vibrations that filled the air of the tent, as in the pain and isolation of creatures who've abandoned their nests, who've left behind all the rest of their kind, forever.

As she began to understand its pain, Girat felt herself grow closer to the visitor, and she sensed the ambiguity in the visitor's mind concerning the exchange of warmth and the reproduction of his species. Very different from her associations concerning the two functions. To Girat, there was no relationship between gene sharing and mind sharing. She projected that thought to the visitor, and felt him drowsily agree to the idea of sharing. Their minds and bodies moved together.

Lying stretched out on the floor of the tent, she shared her breath with him, breathed the air as it came from his body. Their muscles moved together, their limbs glided over each other.

Girat could feel the pain leaving his mind, the edges of his regret dulling. Slowly, she pushed further into his unconscious. He would be left with a sense of loss, which is a worthy emotion, but would no longer feel such pain and longing for his Earth. She spoke to the visitor in words for the first time since they had touched.

"This is a suitable happening for the end of a deathflight. I am honored."

She was lying against him on her chest, one arm over his shoulder, the other reaching forward beyond their heads, her hand curved back toward her face, her long fingers lightly flexed. Alex smiled sleepily. He should find this experience a lot stranger than he did.

Instead, he felt comfortable on this planet for the first time since they'd arrived. He'd been welcomed by one of Pyerva's own people, and they could explore their differences and their similarities. What a wealth of information she could give him.

She rose up slightly on one arm, turned to face him. "This is a suitable happening for the end of a deathflight," she said. "I am honored."

"What is a deathflight?" asked Alex. Perhaps this would explain the mummified birds in the cities.

She sat up slowly. "When we left the cities, thousands of

seasons ago, we left the technology that would support a large population. We must keep our numbers low." Flexing her wings slightly, she stretched her arms out in front of her, tendons and muscles stretching. "So, when a person has accomplished some good and has made a contribution, she is allowed to return to her ancestors' city to die, and one of her eggs is quickened."

This made no sense to Alex. "But why did you leave the cities in the first place? They could support millions."

"The vibrations," she replied. "The cities and their electronics produced vibrations —" she touched his arm, and he associated the word with the electromagnetic spectrum, "—that scar the mind and damage the body. Some people — my ancestors — could feel them, like a sickness, eating at them. They left the cities, got as far away from them as they could, and settled in the rock eyries where we live now. Most people stayed in the cities until it was too late. Perhaps they couldn't feel the vibrations, or perhaps they ignored them. They did not live healthily until death, and their young suffered even more." She paused. "It's time that I left," she said, rising slowly from the floor of the tent, drawing Alex up with her. "If I rest too much, I'll be unable to die properly."

Alex stood stunned for an instant as her meaning sank in, then turned incredulous. He was just beginning to put the pieces together, and there was much more they should talk about. She couldn't die now. She couldn't abandon him.

He grabbed her arms, to keep her in the tent until she regained her senses.

When he grabbed her, Girat instinctively pushed back, but she was too weak to have any effect: almost all her remaining strength was in the muscles that controlled her wings. With a violence of emotion that blew through her mind like a wind, he objected to her leaving, objected to her dying, and threatened to prevent her from continuing her deathflight.

Girat had never found herself in violent opposition to another intelligence. She was totally without referent. She could accept the impersonal barbarity of her environment, she could comprehend searing pain and transmute it. Those were natural occurrences: she could transcend them. But the artificial constraint of one person by another, this was beyond acceptance and comprehension.

He couldn't intend to keep her here! He couldn't place his mind and power in opposition to hers! What kind of incomprehensible monsters were these aliens?

Incredulity and rage burned reason from her mind. She shook uncontrollably. There were other ways of dying. She'd accept a hasty death on the ground before she'd be kept alive against her will.

Suddenly she stopped. The cause of his irrational behavior was available to her: he couldn't understand what she was thinking, he couldn't *hear* her, even when they were touching. She thought again what a lonely, comfortless existence these creatures must lead. But she could project. As long as they were touching, she could put parts of her mind into his, just as she could project words from a distance.

And she did. She projected pure emotion, tied tenuously to facts: the triumph of heroes of her clan who had died beautiful deaths, the pride of her mother, dying that she might live, the joy of the child that would receive life when she was dead. The visitor stopped holding her, but she kept the flow of emotion pouring into him: she relived the euphoria of her deathflight, and felt again an eager anticipation of her death.

When her desire for death became unbearable, she left him.

The next day and the day after, Alex Zamyatin went out into the city despite the heat. It was much too large a city for one man to cover in a day. On the third day, he found her.

It was early, an hour or two past dawn, and the city was rosy with light. She lay, wings spread, in the shadows at the edge of a plaza. She'd been dead for some time.

Her wings, dry as parchment, were loosely outstretched, covering most of her body and the ground around it. One arm lay hidden under her; the other reached forward, her hand near her face, fingers curved slightly inward — the same sleepy pose she had taken in the tent.

Her face was peaceful, what he could see of it. Membranes obscured her large, luminous eyes. She looked, deceptively, as though she were breathing. He could almost see a slight rise and fall of her chest.

He knelt beside her, reached out a hand. Not to move her; she was perfect, careless, spent. He touched the downy leather of her wing, surprised against his will by its coolness. Her flesh, waxy under his fingertips, was colder than he could have anticipated. Dead.

He stroked her wing again, involuntarily. It was difficult to stop, he felt such joy. ⸗

"Contact" is an early story, started in 1976, and finished at the Clarion Writers' Workshop and later at the monthly workshops that Kate Wilhelm and Damon Knight held in Eugene. It's a story with a learning curve: I intentionally worked against my own stylistic preferences, and focused on exploring a number of issues that continue to hold my interest.

I'm afraid that it looks small when juxtaposed with its ambitions, but it's one of those stories where the writer's reach exceeds her grasp. Learning to do that – upping the ante – is exactly what Clarion is for.

The story was bought by Jim Baen for *Destinies*. It was one of a bunch of purchases that he eventually spun out into a separate anthology, called *Proteus*. Sort of a Salon des Refusées of *Destinies*, *Proteus* included stories by Michael Swanwick, George Alec Effinger, and Charles Sheffield. These were mostly character-centered stories by writers with literary ambition, defining rather clearly the aesthetic that Baen did not want, and I was pleased that my story was included.

What Are Friends For?

THE DAY THE NEW THROPO hits Pomona, me and the guys lay a cherry bomb on him, just to show we're glad he came.

Then when he comes down from the palm tree (heyzus, can those snakeheads jump), we tell him it's a, uh, local custom.

"Most hospitable," he says. "Must show you a few of our customs some day." The tentacles where his head should be are wriggling like crazy. He looks like a clothespin wearing a nest of snakes, and he sounds like a mucken 3v announcer.

He sits down next to us on the curb and starts asking us what we do, where we live, all the old jakweb.

We got a couple hours to kill before we hit the condo we been casing, so we scag him around a while. I say I test birth control shots. Chico says he's an assistant breather for DivAirQual. You know.

The thropo swallows everything. Doesn't blink an eye. (And he's got a few extra eyes to blink.) His tentacles quiet down while he listens. After a while the joke bennies and we burn it. Then we just sit around for a couple minutes and look at each other. Finally the thropo gets up and he shakes himself like a dog and he says, "Well, you young people seem to have a very high collective imagination index. Just the sort of thing I've been looking for. Have a pleasant afternoon." Then he walks off.

Later on, after we finish the job (which goes off smooth as high grade hash), we catch him down to Paco's store on the corner. He's over by the magazine rack, checking out the skinnies, taking notes on a little pocket corder. I don't get what he's saying, but he looks pretty worked up for a snakehead.

Allie pokes me in the back. "Hey," she says, "you think they go for that kind of stuff? I thought they laid eggs or something."

"I dunno," I say. "Maybe he's just finding out what he's missing."

"We ought to get old Margie on his ass," says Chico. "She'd teach him a thing or two."

"Shit," says Allie, "even Margie wouldn't do it with a snakehead."

Then he sees us, and all his little tentacles wave. We kind of look at each other. Then we figure what the hell and go over. "A most unusual concept," says the thropo as we get closer. "Portraying the distribution of genetic information in a social context to stimulate the economy."

We look at each other again. "You want stimulating, you should see the live shows down on South Garey," says Allie.

"That would be most instructive," says the thropo. "Perhaps you would all like to accompany me?"

"Shit, man," says Chico, "it costs ten bucks to get in."

"My discretionary fund was intended for such contingencies," says the thropo. We just look at him, and he says, "My treat."

So pretty soon we're sitting in the Pink Flamenco on South Garey, around these tables with bug candles on them, and I'm thinking that this is a pretty screwy thing to be doing, going to a skinshow with a snakehead. The other thropos, they come sniffing around, ask you a few questions, and you give them all the wrong answers. After a while they go away, whether we fool them or not.

But fuck 'em, I say, with their questions and their clinics and their rules and regulations. Sign up here, look over there, pee into this, cough, and let's have a sample of your blood. I don't see where that gets anybody. And it was the same with the government, before the invasion. I mean, a lot of people were really racked out when the snakeheads took over, and a lot of other people said it was a good thing, but to me it's all politics, and whether it's snakeheads or shitheads don't make much difference. So when they send their thropos around asking a lot of dumbass questions like a bunch of snakey little missionaries, I like to give them a hard time. And I don't really understand what I'm doing at the old Flamenco with the new thropo, if you see what I mean.

Just as I'm thinking all this, the show starts. The same tired old farts doing the same tired old numbers they was doing when me and Allie used to sneak in as kids. So we're whistling and yelling and throwing condoms and popcorn at the stage. Then I look over at the thropo, who is sitting next to me, and see that he's taking notes again on his corder.

"What do you use all that stuff for anyway," I say.

"Well," says the thropo, "most of it goes straight into the central processor for reduction and comparative analysis. Be used later in your species evaluation."

"Oh," I say. The double-jointed brother-and-sister act is on stage now, so I return my attention to the show. The thropo goes on snuffling into his corder.

When the DJs are through, I start wondering what the thropo means. Our species evaluation? "What species evaluation?" I say.

"Evaluation by our population control board," he says. "Individuals selected will be transferred to an unoccupied planet. More than enough to go around — hardly seems worth renovating this one."

I am for the moment speechless.

But the thropo's not. "You and your friends have, if I may say so, an excellent chance of being transferred, for your genetic variety ratings are good, your collective imagination score is high, and you demonstrate ability to survive in the face of a hostile environment." He waves his tentacles to include the Flamenco, the valley, the whole state of Los Angeles. "The wealthier castes, I'm afraid, are less adaptable. Deprive them of bodyguards, and they wouldn't last an hour on the streets."

My voice returns. "What happens to the people who stay here?"

"Not my department. Assume they'll be scrapped with the planet. Can't allow them to continue breeding like this, cause trouble in no time."

The double-jointed twins are back, but I'm not in the mood. "Whose idea is this, anyway?"

"Oh," says the thropo, "it's standard procedure. All the new planets are stabilized at a healthful population level where proper aesthetic conditions can be maintained. Never any trouble after that."

No, I think, there wouldn't be.

"When's all this get underway?" I ask.

The thropo shrugs his back and all his tentacles ripple. "Doing the best we can. Genetic studies have been completed, of course, but the evaluation process can't start until the anthropological studies are ready. Afraid you could be here another week."

"A week? Shit, man, that don't give us much time to pack." I am thinking I don't mind being among the chosen few, but I am not so sure I want to be trucked off to some other planet. I mean, I was in Michigan once, and once was enough. But I figure there's nothing I can do about it right now, so I decide to relax and glom the show.

"Ain't that blonde a whiff?" I say to the thropo, just to be friendly.

"Marvelous, simply marvelous," says the thropo. "A shame that such things must come to an end, but then, as one of your poets has put it so beautifully—"

"What come to an end?" I say. "What's that supposed to mean?"

"Oh, there will be programs recorded on holotape in the museums. No need to worry that it will all be completely lost."

"Completely lost?" I say, beginning to sound like a looped holotape myself. "What will be completely lost?"

"Nothing, as I say," says the thropo. "But naturally, after the conversion process, this sort of thing will no longer be commercially feasible. It's to be expected that there will be some changes in the economic milieu as a result of the migration. But this is such an unusual approach to the peripheral economic situation—an entire industry devoted to depicting the mechanics of evolution and species survival, millions of people dependent upon it for their livelihood, you understand—that I think it's worth recording, if only as a galactic cultural curiosity. One of my little projects this trip."

I start off at the place where I got lost. "What conversion process?"

"The neuterization process," he says. "Don't want your new planet to turn into a grossly overpopulated mess like this one. Our genetically-tailored recombinant replacement process yields all the benefits of Type III distribution, and it's really much more reliable than the cumbersome organic method."

I get just about every other word, but I get the drift. "Neuter?" I say. "You're not going to fucking neuter *me*."

"Ah," says the thropo. "English semantic structure can sometimes be most confusing."

I am about to tell him what he can do with his confusion, but I figure I should cruise it a bit. "This, uh, neuterization process," I say, "uh, how'd you say it works?" Meantime I'm thinking maybe I should watch the show more carefully, because in a little while I might not be interested in this sort of thing at all.

"Automatic," says the thropo. "Just wonderful, the equipment we have now. When I first started out, we had to do it all by hand, you know."

"No, no," say. "I mean, do you, you know, *cut* anything? Or is it, uh—"

"Ah," he says. "Nothing like that. Just a spot of directed radiation and of course a psychic implant. Inhibits the libido and prevents wasteful energy loss."

This new angle makes it pretty difficult for me to just sit and watch the show, let me tell you. I mean, who wants to be turned into a zombie and sent off to some weird planet? But those snakeheads, there's no fooling around with them. The thropos, they don't give you any trouble, but you don't mess with their cops. Those people who fought the snakeheads really got fried.

After the show, we ditch the thropo and I tell the guys what he says. This causes some surprise, as you can imagine. The first question is, how come he told it to me, when nobody else seems to have heard about it. Now, I can't really answer that, except maybe other people know and they're not telling. But I convince the guys that what I'm telling them is true. I don't lie to the guys, they know that.

Everybody agrees that life on this new planet, whatever it's like, would be a hustle and a half compared to life on Pomona. This is despite the fact, which you may not know, that it's tough to make a living as a nixen these days. Most of the greeners are pretty dumb, but they got these fuckin' defense systems you need a goddam degree in engineering to get past.

We figure we're going to have to do something fast. But we don't know what.

So the next day we've got a lookout for the thropo and we catch him standing in line to see a triple feature at the Magnafox, a bunch of Japanese spleebies with titles like *Sex Sluts From Beyond the Universe*. He's got his holocorder with him.

We mumble him a little, then we lead him around to what we want to know.

"Who's in charge of this neuterization program, anyway?" I ask, real casual.

"In this sector?" says the thropo. "I am. And I can tell you, it's not a job that leaves me much time for field research."

I don't have much sympathy for his troubles, but I am very happy to learn that we know the guy in charge. The thropo, however, doesn't stop there.

"The subtleties of your reproduction ritual and the multiplicity of commercial media depicting its forms leave me with little hope of observing all types of socio-sexual economic interaction first hand." The thropo waves a tentacle or two at the theater billboard, which is a full-color holoposter of this blonde whiff who is wearing antennas on her head and very little else, being threatened by an ugly-looking monster with a huge dick. When you move, the monster leers and shakes his dick. "When one considers," says the thropo, "the interpolation of additional thematic content, such as the exploitation of your species' regrettable xenophobia, the amount of material is simply overwhelming."

I am beginning to see some possibilities. "You need time, huh?" I say. "This isn't something you can do after we move to this new planet?"

"The social context is most important," says the thropo. "Of course, we are assembling great collections of source material — films, photos, printed matter, ritual clothing and devices. But after neuterization, the social context will be lost forever. The other day, for instance, when you and your friends were participating in the performance, tossing objects to the performers and interacting with them, I noticed that many of the other people there, the older men especially, were most introspective.

I want to examine that sort of reaction as well, but I simply can't be everywhere at once."

The line is getting closer to the door, and I can see that if I don't get the thropo away, I'm going to lose him entirely. So I talk the thropo into skipping the spleebie for now and joining us in a bar across the street. The bar is the pits, hot and dark, with air that's been resyked so many times it has garlic on its breath. But I figure at least the thropo will buy the cervesa, so it won't be a total loss, even if he doesn't buy my line.

We all cram in around a dirty little table in the corner and I start my rap. "You need time, huh?" I say. "You're the Man, how come you don't just make time?"

"So many planets," says the thropo. "So much material to collect. If I thought the subject important enough, I'd stay here a while, research it more thoroughly. Someday, perhaps, I may wish I had. Difficult to judge."

"If you stay here," I say, "will you still be sending people to that other planet?"

"Certainly not," says the thropo. "Need everyone here. No meaningful research can be done with the remnants of a planet's population. But I see little justification for staying. Nothing that would convince my superiors, at any rate."

"There's lots of stuff," I say, "that you haven't seen at all. You just hit the shelves, man. There's stuff behind the counter, too, you know. And nobody'd show it to a thropo." I look over to Chico, who I know I can count on to get things right the first time. "Chico," I say, "run down and get some UC zines from Paco. Rubber, S-and-M, chickens, watersports, whatever you can find." I look back at the thropo. "You'll see lots you never seen before."

While we're waiting for Chico, I want to keep the thropo busy, so I ask him what he gets off on most.

"Oh, it all fascinates me," he says. "Just the thought, for one thing, that humans would be interested in watching the mating ritual, when survival theory indicates they should be more interested in participating. How does a watcher maintain its genetic strain in competition with those who exchange germ plasm more readily?" He looks around at us, as if he thinks we can answer this. "In addition," he says, "there's the use of this voyeuristic tendency, however it's inherited, as a means of generating employment. Not only the people who produce this material, but their suppliers, distributors, those who sell them office and living space, these people all benefit. It's a very valuable service. If there were no demand for it, there would be millions more starving." He goes on like this for a while, and I am hatching out what I'm going to do when Chico comes back. I figure I will continue to play it by ear, because the thropo seems pretty good at selling himself on whatever he wants to buy.

Finally Chico turns up, and he's got a good bunch of zines with him. The thropo is high as Jamaica.

"Most unusual material," he says, and he's muttering other stuff to himself in a sort of snuffle. "Here, for instance, the sub-jugation of violence to the purposes of procreation." He flips through another stack. "A paradoxical denial of the generative religious cult to further the process of generation." I don't know where Paco sells all this stuff showing people dressed like nuns, but somebody must buy it. "And these magazines seem to spe-cialize in the use of devices that —" He goes on and on.

"So what's the word?" I say. "You think we're worth studying a little longer?"

The thropo looks up. "Yes," he says. "I feel quite confident that my superiors would approve a few decades of intensive research. Perhaps more, dependent on results."

"So you'll be around for quite a while," I say. Another idea is getting to me. "You could probably use some help. Me and Allie here, and Tom and Rita and Chico and LaVerne, we'll be glad

to show you where the *real* action is. We don't charge much."
I figure we won't have it too hard, getting paid to find the thropo
some action. And I am keeping in mind that business has been
lousy lately, like I said.

The thropo gets all choked up. "I don't know how to show my
appreciation for all this," he says. "It could be the making of my
reputation. The preservation of cultural treasures like these and
the retention of their social context. And they could so easily
have been destroyed with your planet."

"Relax," I say. "We're your friends, right? What are friends
for if they can't help you out once in a while?" By this time the
thropo is almost crying, if snakeheads can cry. He falls all over us
with his snakey thanks and pays for the beers, like I thought. ⸕

This was my first published story, aside from a few early efforts in a college
literary magazine. It was bought by Ted White for *Amazing Stories*, way back
in 1978.

As a kid, I haunted the news store in my hometown for the digest-sized
science-fiction magazines that sporadically appeared. *Amazing* and its sis-
terzine *Fantastic* were my favorites, as they had the most extreme covers
— mutants and sexy spacebabes.

My story, appropriately, was published with a striking black-and-white
illustration depicting the snakehead and a randomly-assigned buxom
young lady, who is not in the story. (I loved it. The artist, a newcomer
named Rodak, seems to have vanished without a trace. If you're out there,
Rodak, get in touch.)

My check for $51.63 came from the publisher, Sol Cohen, a few months
later -- in someone else's stamped self-addressed envelope, with their name
crossed out and mine scrawled in above it. I had hit the big time.

Ideologically Labile Fruit Crisp

Fruit mixture:

    4 to 6 cups of berries or manipulated fruit

    2 tablespoons tart juice (optional)

    1 to 2 pinches spice (optional)

    1 to 2 teaspoons thickener (optional)

    2 to 12 tablespoons sweetener (optional)

Crunchy stuff:

    1 to 2 tablespoons flour

    1/2 cup (or more) nuts or seeds

    1 cup crushed cereal or crumbs

    1/4 to 3/4 cup oil or shortening

    1 to 2 pinches spice (optional)

    1/4 to 1 teaspoon salt (also optional)

    2 to 12 tablespoons sweetener (very optional)

Put the fruit mixture in a casserole. Mix the crunchy stuff in a bowl, making sure the oil or shortening gets distributed throughout. Put the crunchy stuff on top of the fruit. Bake in a 375-degree oven until the fruit bubbles and the top browns. Serve on plates, with something cold and white.

This recipe strives to be ideologically neutral, and can be adapted to please most castes, creeds, pocketbooks, and political persuasions. It's too messy to sell at a bake sale.

PART II | EXPLICATION DE TEXTE

First, define your agenda. Leftwing, rightwing, or middle-American? Yuppie or blue-collar? Healthfood or junkfood? Cuisine minceur, grosseur, ou farceur? Take into consideration any special-interest groups, such as 5-year-olds.

Next, choose your fruit. Fresh, frozen, canned, or dried? You can choose something plentiful and cheap, or conspicuously expensive. You can pick it yourself, or buy fruit picked by someone else. In the latter case, you might wonder who picked it and what their lives are like. Or you might not.

Manipulate the fruit as necessary to remove seeds, stems, and stones, and to make it cook more quickly. This usually involves cutting or slicing it. You can peel it or not, whichever is most compatible with your aesthetic and digestive systems. If you're feeling really obsessive, you can peel it, core it, and cut it into 3/8-inch-wide slices. (If you find you want to peel and slice berries, you should call your therapist for assistance.)

We won't deconstruct your choice of casserole: it may simply be the only ovenproof dish you have that is big enough. If you think cooked fruit adheres stubbornly to baking dishes, you can rub the inside of the casserole with a congealed fatty substance. When you put the fruit in the dish, you might want to arrange it in concentric circles. Then again, you might not.

You may now mix the following optional substances with the fruit or, if you've arranged the fruit in a pattern, pour them on top of it.

Tart liquid: Fresh or bottled lemon or lime juice, frozen orange juice concentrate, or vinegar. Do any of these choices make you uncomfortable? Why?

Spice: Cinnamon, nutmeg, and allspice are conventional; cardamom, clove, ginger, or mace are more daring. Using all of them is foolhardy.

Thickener: Flour, cornstarch, or instant tapioca. Mix this well with the fruit. If you've arranged the fruit in a pattern, skip the thickener, because it will lie glutinously in a layer, like the economic benefits of tax breaks for the rich.

Sweetener: Your most ideologically sensitive decision. Sugar (white, brown, raw, turbinado), honey (processed, raw, comb), maple syrup, molasses, brown rice syrup, barley malt extract, Karo syrup (light or dark), sorghum syrup, treacle, fruit preserves, raisins, dates, or gummi bears. (Do any of these disgust you? How come? Health? Politics? Class or ethnic origins? Age-group? Trendiness-index?) Add as much or as little sweetener as you can tolerate. For assistance, consult your priest or shaman, or in an emergency, call 911.

Now we come to the crunchy stuff. You really have an opportunity to express yourself here. ("You was always crazy, Thelma," said Louise. "You just never had a chance to express yourself before.") Below are some of your choices.

Flour: Bleached white, stoneground whole wheat, defatted soybean.

Nuts: Almonds, walnuts, pecans, hazelnuts, cashews, peanuts, shredded coconut, sunflower seeds.

Cereals: Rolled oats, wheatgerm, granola, cornflakes, anything that comes free in the mail with a 25-cents-off coupon.

Crumbs: From stale bread or cake, graham crackers, cookies, macaroons, or those salt-free Triskets that somebody brought to your New Year's Eve Party in 1987.

Oil or shortening: Butter, peanut or safflower oil, sesame oil, even (gasp!) Crisco. (But not olive oil! No! No! No!)

Salt: Sea salt, kosher salt, iodized free-flowing table salt, salt-free salt.

Okay. You've made your choices and baked your dessert. Now choose what you're going to put on top of it. Whipped cream? Yogurt? Crème fraîche? Yaourt? Tofu-based frozen dessert-supplement? Yoghourt? Cool Whip? Yoghert? Ack! Maybe I'll just have a Pepperidge Farm cookie and a glass of milk. ⬩

Spring Conditions

MIA PUSHED HERSELF SLOWLY to the top of the rise on her long, narrow skis. She was still hung over and wrung out from last night, and though the hill was not steep, it required all the effort she wanted to give. When she got to the ridge, she waited there for Zeb.

The day was wet and too warm, the forest dripping, fog-muffled, monochromatic. The snow, heavy and granular beneath her skis, was still three or four feet deep. Dead sticks thrust out of it. Light rain fell with a distant murmur, like the sound of a silk shroud.

The top of the hill was only sparsely covered with trees, and she could see further ahead, where the trail sloped down to a small, snow-covered pond. It was darker down there, and a damp breeze was rising from the pond. Mia shivered. Warm air moves uphill; she had read that somewhere. Warm air moving uphill can be a storm signal in the Sierras. Or was that just at night?

They'd have to start back to the lodge soon, but maybe they'd have time to check out the pond. It would be a nice place to hike to later in the spring, but, like the woods along the trail, it was sad and decayed now. The death of winter is the first sign of spring in the Sierras, but winter here doesn't die easy.

Mia felt a small death in her, too: the first indication, perhaps, of a rebirth. Skiing, solitary, ahead of Zeb, she had come to a decision. Her anger of last night had dissipated, but like the alcohol that had fed it, it had left her feeling sick. They had fought so many times before, over such insignificant matters. It was time to put an end to it.

Zeb skied up beside her. Brown, bearded, not unfriendly in spite of their fight, he was a welcome sight, but Mia hardened her resolve.

"Porcupine tracks back there," he said, slightly out of breath. "Like someone dragged a broom across the snow."

"I've made a decision," said Mia. "I'm getting out of LA. Maybe go to Oregon." She looked away from him, between two scraggly lodgepole pines, toward the pond.

Zeb stared at her warily. "It wasn't that bad a fight," he said. "I'm sure the staff at the lodge has forgotten all about it. There's no need to leave the state."

Mia smiled slightly, against her will. "I'm serious."

"We shouldn't throw away our time together so casually."

"You mean we should stick it out like a cat and dog tied tail-to-tail?" Mia didn't want to face him. Her eyes sought the distance, the dark woods beyond the far edge of the pond.

"We don't have to fight," said Zeb. He was still looking at her. "I don't even understand what we fought about last night."

Mia forced herself to turn to him, and the courage of honesty came to her. "I don't know, either. There's just something in me that lashes out at you. That's why I want to go. There's something in me that fears and hates and fights, and I have no control over it with you. It's happened before, too, with other people."

Now Zeb searched the forest, refused to meet her eyes. "This is no place to have a serious conversation. We've got to get going anyway, if we're going to make it back to the lodge before dark."

"I want to get a closer look at the pond," said Mia, relieved to drop the subject. She pushed forward on her skis. The corner of the pond that had been hidden by the pines came into view. The surface of the ice was broken, and there was a jagged circle of brown water, as though someone had fallen in. She called out to Zeb.

He came up beside her, and gave a puzzled grunt. "No footprints, no ski tracks. No sign of an animal. Kind of far from the trees for a limb to have fallen in."

The air coming up from the pond was wet and clinging. Mia shivered again. "Maybe something's breaking out," she said. Zeb looked at her blankly; that didn't make sense. "Let's go," she said. "It's getting cold and dark." As she turned to go down the slope the way they'd come, she thought she saw something move in the dark gap of the pond. "Wait." She swung back to see what it was. In the dark brown water, something was bobbing slowly, just under the surface. It was pale and bulky, like a badly wrapped package. A body?

"If it happened before the last snow, there'd be no tracks," said Zeb.

As they watched, the package broke the surface slowly and gently, like a bubble rising in oil. It bobbed uncertainly and rotated. A bare foot, white as chalk, appeared from underneath. The stench of rotting flesh drifted like mist up the slope. There was someone in there, past any help they could give.

"My god," whispered Mia. But Zeb was already heading down the hill to the pond. "What are you going to do?" she shouted. He didn't answer, and she pushed off after him, their argument already far in the past.

She caught up to him quickly. They stopped at the bottom of the hill, by the edge of the pond. They couldn't see the body any better than they had from the hill. Was it wearing a tan parka? The foot had sunk back down below the water: it wasn't visible. The smell of putrefaction was stronger now, almost overwhelming.

"We can't possibly drag it back to the lodge," Mia said.

"I know," said Zeb. "The shape it's in, it would fall apart anyway. But if we can get a look at the clothing, see if there's any identification on it, maybe the rangers will be able to figure out who it was."

"God, this is gruesome."

"Eh. Good an end as any. Bottom of a quiet pond in the Sierras." He was edging out onto the ice.

"Be careful. I couldn't drag you back, either." Now that she was down by the pond, the air felt even wetter, almost slimy. The hole was close to the edge of the pond, only about eight feet away. From close up, it looked larger and somehow hungry. Zeb's skis were leaving long, brown-soaked tracks.

"Give me the tip of your pole to hold on to," he said.

Mia did. "I don't like this," she said. "How can you go out there?"

"If you were in there, you'd want somebody to find out who you were." Zeb's voice was calm, the voice of a man who didn't believe he'd fall in. He was gingerly testing the ice. As he moved, the body bobbed. His weight was bouncing the ice on the water like a raft. Mia winced.

Zeb moved further out onto the ice, still holding onto Mia's pole, and she moved up behind him. Her skis were resting mostly on the land, with about two feet of the tips out on the ice. Zeb was all the way out, his weight distributed by his skis.

"I can almost reach it with my pole," he said. "Maybe I can pull it over and grab it."

"I don't like this, Zeb." Fear welled in her throat like vomit.

"There's something else in there!" Another light-colored mass was moving in the brown water, coming out from under the shelf of ice.

Mia pulled back, the hair bristling coldly at the nape of her neck.

"Don't do that!" shouted Zeb angrily.

Ashamed — they were dead bodies, after all — Mia moved out again onto the ice.

Zeb was redistributing his weight, extending his pole to snag the body on the top. There was a sudden splash, and something whipped out of the water and grabbed the pole, just above the round plastic basket at the end. Zeb let go of Mia's pole and without even a yell was pulled into the water.

Mia froze as Zeb disappeared under the surface. She could see more bodies below. Huge and pale, they rose like feeding fish from under the ice. The water began to ripple, then to boil furiously.

Mia yelled. She moved out onto the ice towards the hole, striking at the shapes in the churning water. A long thin hand reached like a tentacle out of the water and grabbed her pole. It was dead white, the skin wrinkled and sloughing off the wet bones. Mia pulled back, but it was too strong. She was losing her balance. She let her hand go limp, and her pole and globe were ripped away. Without thinking, Mia scrambled back for the bank, and landed heavily on her side. The hole in the pond was getting wider; brown patches appeared in the snow-covered ice and sank away into open water. There were more things trying to get out.

At the edge of the pond, she hesitated, stunned. It had happened so quickly. Zeb was still in there. Could he still be alive?

More holes opened in the ice and more claw-like hands grasped toward her. The water in the pond lapped at her skis. It was rising.

Faster than her brain, her body acted. When she snapped to, she was already half-way up the hillside, with no idea of how she'd gotten that far. She kept going, moving almost straight up the slope.

When she got to the top, she stopped, but didn't look back.

Were there sounds behind her? She was paralyzed momentarily: her need to get away fought with a sense of duty. She should go back down to the pond and find Zeb.

The soft sounds behind her got louder. She didn't look back, but pushed off down the hill toward the lodge. Two sets of tracks went up the hill, only one was going back down. Mia forced herself to concentrate on her skiing.

After an interminably long time, pushing herself through the darkening forest, she swung onto the logging road that led toward the lodge. She pushed her way ahead with long skating strokes; it was a low, easy grade downhill. There were no more noises behind her. But was that a soft slithering in the trees to the right? Just the wind? She refused to listen.

What had really happened, she asked herself. Could she have helped Zeb? Was there anything she could have done? Would the rangers believe her if she told them, or should she make up a story that made more sense?

There couldn't have been live things in that pond. Maybe Zeb had caught his pole on some weeds, and the ice cracked and collapsed. She should have kept her head, and pulled him out. She had killed him by panicking.

The sound in the trees had passed her — just the wind after all. Mia knew she couldn't have helped Zeb. She pushed her body harder. A muscle throbbed in her thigh. She ignored it.

She came to a small meadow, with young pines freckling its edge in the fog, and Mia recognized the last steep grade before the lodge. It was almost dark and she was tiring. She wasn't good on steep hills, even when she was fresh, and with only one pole, she wasn't balanced properly. She pushed her heels down and dug in the edges of her skis going around the narrow curves. She didn't slow down.

She could see the lights up ahead now, hear the clanging of the yard-bell that helped skiers get their bearing in the fog. She dreaded arriving at the lodge. She dreaded having to tell anyone what had happened.

The logging road opened into the clearing, and Mia finally broke free of the forest. She was certain that nothing was following her: nothing had ever been following her. She stopped and looked back. There were no sounds behind or beside her, and she could see nothing moving.

Mia wanted to turn around and go back to the pond, to find Zeb and pull him out of the water, to breathe life back into him. She wanted to make right everything she had done wrong. It had been the anger inside her that had killed him, the force that lashed out at people close to her. Mia wasn't crying, but her face was wet with tears, and they kept coming, as if they belonged to someone else.

She faced back towards the lodge and pushed off, but there were no lights up ahead now. Power failure? It was almost too dark to see, but the trail was still a lighter tone than the forest.

Suddenly, the outside lights of the lodge came on again. She was very close, just a few hundred yards more. It had started to snow, and the lights illumined the heavy flakes as they fell slowly. But there were still no lights on inside the lodge.

She skied closer, staring at the dark picture windows that faced the beginners' slope. There was nobody inside, and it was very quiet. In the snow near the door, there were long brush marks, as though somebody had dragged a broom across it.

Mia peered into the windows. She had trouble focusing her eyes at first. Inside she could see huge, pale shapes bobbing slowly against the panes. Ragged bits of flesh and detritus swam in the air as in soup. Zeb floated there with the rest of them, his skin white and puckered, his eyes open and unseeing, his jaw slack. Aimlessly, as if on a current, he was drifting closer to the window.

These things wanted her. They were a part of her already

— perhaps they had come from her. She would see this through to the end.

Mia skied over to the doorway and stopped. She tapped the toe clamps with her pole, and stepped out of the skis. Then she opened the door and went inside. ⸱

One day, early in 1981, my ever-helpful father called to tell me that Stephen King was judging a short-story contest for the *Boston Phoenix*, and I should enter. I had never written horror, but I was looking, as usual, for a deadline that would propel me through a story.

A few years before, I had had a vivid dream of watching from a height as a corpse's foot broke through from beneath a frozen pond, and it seemed destined for a horror story. I chose a cross-country skiing setting because it seemed to work against the grain of horror, so maybe the material would not be too shopworn. I tried to write a story that would please both Stephen King and myself. Writing the story took the full six weeks allotted and gave me nightmares, but I finished it by the deadline and sent it off.

A few weeks later, I got a letter from the *Boston Phoenix* thanking me for entering and telling me I had finished in the top 1000. I envision them buried in thousands of really bad horror stories. Stephen King, of course, read a few that were filtered from the ocean of entries and chose a winner. This was pretty much what I had expected, and I wasn't particularly crushed. Hey, now I had written three stories, and in only, what, six years? The pace left me breathless.

Jessica Amanda Salmonson bought the story for her anthology *Tales By Moonlight*, and, bless her heart, she persuaded Stephen King to write the introduction. King wrote a generous-spirited essay – most of the contributors were new writers – and it was enormously heartening to me to find out that, not only had Stephen King finally read the story that I had written specifically to please him, but that he actually *liked* it. Thank you, Stephen.

Nota bene: My partner, the very same John D. Berry who designed the volume you hold in your hand, also wrote a story for the *Boston Phoenix* contest. He finished in the top 500, and won a paperpack Stephen King book. Jessica took his story as well.

Nirvana High

Eileen Gunn & Leslie What

SUNDAY MORNING. Barbara awoke from a Technicolor dream in which she was holding hands with the sexiest person in the universe (though the person's head was blank and fuzzy, and she was afraid it might be a girl instead of a boy) and dove straight into a vision predicting her chemistry teacher's death. Barbara watched the accident unfold as it would happen that night: Mrs. Rathbone, dressed in her scarlet microfiber inflatable-bra-and-bustle outfit with spangles and silver fringe, was going to teleport from the Microsoft Park marina to Microsoft Stadium on the other side of the lake. It would be a fundraiser for the basketball team at Cobain High, which meant that nobody Barbara knew would attend. Special-ed students didn't do team sports.

The textile-arts class had added the fringe and spangles on Friday to get extra credit. Everyone was nervous, especially Mrs. R. She had never tried to teleport so far in public before.

Barbara never knew the why of things that she foresaw, so she wasn't sure if it was the distance or maybe some kind of interference from the spangles and fringe that would cause Mrs. Rathbone to rematerialize surrounded by a hundred cubic meters of frigid lake water, flooding the stadium.

Not that it mattered: she couldn't change the outcome anyway. She lay in bed, in the room she shared with her younger sister, holding the dread inside and ignoring the details of what she had just seen. Mrs. R was the only person she liked in the entire school.

Eventually her alarm clock went off, its tiny voice soft and insinuating: "B.J., this is the beginning of a wonderful new day! It's truly lovely weather outside, and today's Sunday, a great day to develop the extrovert in your personality!" It sounded like her mother, and its voice got louder and more insistently cheery if she ignored it. "Barbara! If you get up right now, you can —" She whacked it with the heel of her hand and it shut up. Her sister was already downstairs watching cartoons. She had begun before dawn and would continue until bedtime, pausing only for commercials. Sometimes the whole cartoon was a commercial.

Barbara washed her face and carefully shaved designs in her scalp with a tiny electric razor. She hoped it looked okay: she couldn't really see what she was doing in the back. She put more glue on the dreads, just in case. Then she got dressed and went down to the kitchen for breakfast.

"Well, good morning, B.J.," said her mother. "You're up early for Sunday. That new alarm clock must be *working*, hey?" Her mother looked at her hair, started to say something, then reconsidered. Instead, she grabbed Barbara's wrists, turned them over, and inspected them in the sunlight. "You can hardly see the scars now." She nodded in satisfaction. "I'm so glad we went ahead with the plastic surgery. Your father was wrong — it's certainly worth the extra money."

"Waste of dough, Mom," said Barbara. "Scars rule."

Her mother let go of her. "This bacon your father got for breakfast — I worry about the sodium content. On the *Today Show* they were talking about sodium and nitrous in packaged meats. It causes cancer."

"Nitrates, Mom. Nitrous is what you inhale." But her mother was already off on another subject, spouting some completely incomprehensible psychobabble she'd heard on TV that morning. "Mom, was I adopted?" Her mother didn't answer.

Throughout the day, Barbara did her best to keep her mind off her premonition, so her parents wouldn't notice anything unusual. They were worried enough about her self-esteem, without her troubling them with something real. Mostly she stayed in her room, listening to Airhead real loud on the phones and trying to figure out the words.

At dinner, she picked at her food: soggy ramen noodles with overcooked peapods and undercooked carrots. For dessert, a kiwi-fruit-flavored Jello with embedded banana slices. The jello had achieved a colloidal state, and the banana slices hung suspended in light-green goo. It reminded her of chemistry class. She pushed it away and excused herself from the table.

"You didn't take very much to eat," said her mother. "You've been awfully quiet."

Barbara groaned and pulled on her jacket. "I'm going to the basketball fundraiser," she said. She didn't really want to go, but she had to be there. She had to see what happened.

"Dressed like that?" asked her father. "What the hell did you do to your hair?"

"That's nice," said her mother quickly. "You make some friends who like basketball. That's a *good* idea."

She figured she'd go to the marina, where Mrs. R was starting from. The crowds would be at the stadium, waiting for her to reappear.

Barbara knew there was nothing she could do. When she was a kid, when she first started premoting, she tried to change things. She told her father not to eat at the JellyBelly Deli, but her remark whetted his appetite for knishes; he got salmonella. She told her sister not to get up on the high slide, but Tina didn't like being ordered around; she broke her arm. The incident with her mother's car was especially unfortunate.

Barbara caught on, and now kept her mouth shut — it didn't make any difference in the results, but at least she didn't get blamed for it. She had never premoted anything this serious before, but she knew what she had to do: stay out of the way of the inevitable.

At the marina, a platform had been set up overlooking Lake Washington, with a field of folding chairs in front of it. Most of the chairs were empty, except way up near the stage. Barbara sat on the side in the back and tried to look invisible.

Klieg lights were waving through the sky, and cameras from the school TV station were trained on Mrs. R's presumed trajectory, although no one had ever been observed in the act of teleportation. Huge screens from the Microsoft–Sony Educational Channel had been set up to make the experience of being there as real as watching it on TV. The Cobain Marching Band was on the platform playing the school song, "Live Through This." The drum majors, dressed as Courtney Love, screamed out the lyrics. The norms really made a big deal of all this fascist school-spirit stuff. Barbara wondered how they faked it.

She moved quickly into a seat at the back, leaving a space between herself and a skinny geek with a scramble of hair at the top. He looked like a spesh — funny she didn't know him.

And then, there she was on the screen, bigger than life: Mrs. R, spangles twinkling, silver fringe fluttering. She'd obviously been given a heavy dusting of glitter just before taking the stage, and she left a shimmery trail behind her, like a slug.

Cobain's principal, Mr. Madonna, an XXY with extra-high intuitive qualities and an inclination to hold pep rallies, introduced her, though he said she needed no introduction, then led the band in a medley of sentimental grunge. Barbara loathed grunge.

And then Mrs. R stepped forward very quietly and started to, well, ripple. She wavered, like hot air on the highway in August.

In her dream, Barbara had seen all the details: the water, the noise, the rush of people to the exits, Mrs. R's cold, white, limp body lying alone on the stage afterward.

The reality was worse. The audience at the stadium was really spooked, not to mention they got wet. The CPR team entered the hall cautiously, and way too late. At Microsoft Park, the audience couldn't figure out what was going on. The guy next to her couldn't seem to believe it. He kept saying, "This is incredible!" over and over again. Finally he turned to Barbara and asked, "Why did she do herself like that in front of everybody?" Barbara got up out of her seat and walked away.

He followed her, still babbling. "She's the oldest spesh I've ever seen. She must have been one of the first. If she held out that long, what made her crack?"

"She didn't do it to herself," Barbara said finally. Mrs. R wouldn't have. She was sane. She was happy. She couldn't have done it to herself.

"My God, I hope you're right." He grabbed her elbow. Barbara almost pulled away, but he didn't seem dangerous. "Come on," he said.

She felt the ground beneath her feet fall away, then return. Wooden flooring. It was dark. The guy let go of her elbow. What kind of a nut was he? Where had he taken her? What the fuck was going on? He hit a light switch, and she realized where she was: Mrs. R's chem lab.

"Jesus!"

"Don't be scared: watch." He grabbed a beaker and some flasks from a cabinet. "You take a little of this, a pinch of that. Use your bunsen burner like a blow torch, and —"

"No! I'm outta here!"

The air in the room grew thick with noxious clouds that fizzled and popped and made her nose burn. He grabbed her and pulled her tightly to him, forcing his mouth onto hers. The clouds in the room turned black and heavy, and she couldn't breathe — she couldn't even take a breath. She started to pass out, his mouth on hers, his tongue down her throat. My mother was right, she thought. I shouldn't talk to strange guys.

The next thing she knew, they were back outside the marina. He was still kissing her, and he'd pressed up against her real close. He had a hard-on, and she was kissing him back.

She broke away.

"Did that help?" he said.

"What the fuck is the matter with you?"

"I thought you could use a rush. Like in her honor, you know?"

"You are seriously fucked," said Barbara. "Stay away from me." She ran for the bus.

At the school door on Monday morning, Barbara pushed her right hand against the security switch that verified her ID, scanned her person for possible weapons, and then evaluated her emotional state to determine whether or not she would use them. The twitch switch, they called it. Since they could no longer ban guns, the schools tried to keep out students who would use them irresponsibly.

The solenoid seemed to hesitate. She forced herself to take a deep calm breath and slowly traced the raised lettering with the fingers of her free hand. "Donated by Microsoft–ADT Intrusion Insurance." I am not an intruder, she thought, without feeling. It worked; the switch beeped its discreet little signal, and the door opened to admit her to school.

A norm, by his looks one of the CAS — the criminally active

students—was standing by the lockers. He turned to stare at Barbara as she walked down the hall. The CAs weren't too friendly to the special-skills students. None of the norms were, but the CAs, who sometimes tipped toward the sociopathic end of the scale, worried Barbara more than the other norms. Supposedly every student at Cobain was a suicide risk, but you kind of got the feeling that the CAs might just take you with them.

"Hey, spesh," said the norm, fiddling with a bone-handled folding knife. "Guess what I'm thinking."

Her class was through the first door, and she had to pass him to get there. She put an edge on her voice that was sharper than his knife. "*I'm* thinking you'd look pretty funny with half a dick…. And now *you're* thinking, 'I wonder if she can see into the future,' because that wasn't what you were thinking at all."

The norm looked confused. "Psycho bitch," he muttered, but he turned back to his locker and didn't pursue her as she walked by.

In class, she took her seat at the back of the lab, in the Microsoft–Dow section, still fuming at what jerks norms were. Pretty much everyone had heard about the drowning at Lake Washington; Barbara didn't bother to block it from her mind, even though she usually guarded her thoughts around the telepaths.

Minerva, seated next to her, looked up. "Entertain us!" she called out. "Barbie was *there* when Mrs. Rathbone made like a salmon and went extinct."

Before Barbara could brace herself, almost everyone in the classroom was pushing for a place inside her brain, probing her consciousness with questions like icy fingers. Telepaths froze her nose, the way they plugged in at will.

"Did she die all at once, or was it slow and lingering?"

"Did our test scores die with her?"

"Did her bra fill up with water?"

"Entertain us!"

"Entertain us!"

"Entertain us!"

That was a Cobain thing. It meant one thing to the teachers, another to the students. To the teachers it meant "pay attention." To the students it meant "stop whatever you're doing that's interesting and do what we want you to do." To Kurt Cobain, of course, it had meant "stick a shotgun in your mouth."

All she needed to do was answer. Tell them all the grim details. Make it sound funny, make it sound like she didn't care. If she gave them what they wanted, she'd be one of the gang. So why couldn't she do it?

"Nevermind," Barbie said.

"Did she leave a note?" Minerva asked. She gave a nervous laugh.

"That's not funny," Barbie said. "It was an accident."

The ITV buzzed on and Mr. Madonna spoke to the class.

"Special-skills students," he said, "As most of you know, Mrs. Rathbone met with a tragic accident last night, in the service of Cobain High. I am sure she would want you to quietly resume your studies and to welcome Mr. Collins, who will be with you shortly. We can all be proud of Mrs. Rathbone, because Microsoft–Boeing will be presenting the basketball team with new uniforms in her memory. Grief counseling will be provided in the cafeteria at lunchtime, courtesy of Microsoft–Taco Bell, and there will be a celebration of life sponsored by Microsoft–Coca-Cola on Friday at noon."

"Yeah?" shouted Carl. "What's in it for me?"

Grief counseling probably wasn't going to be necessary for most of the students, because Mrs. R was one of the few special-ed teachers who had the power to control her class, and most of the kids hadn't liked her very much. The other teachers had the psychic strength of fig newtons, but when you gave Mrs. R a hard time, she teleported you straight to detention.

And Barbara had been her pet. There was no denying that: Barbara could have said anything in that class and gotten away with it. This had put her in an awkward predicament. When you can say anything you want, and the teacher takes your questions absolutely seriously and understands what you were really asking and answers *that* question, it's not so much fun to be smartass all the time. It's more interesting to think up really good questions. Especially when you're actually getting interested in the subject. This is what had earned her the nickname "Barbie" in the first place.

"Mrs. Rathbone's Teen-Talk Barbie," Carl had called her when she asked too many questions about chemistry. Just like the Barbie doll that said "Trigonometry is fun! Want some help with it?" and "I find chemistry very stimulating!"

Carl's names for people stuck like birdshit because of the leadership thing: some people had it, most people didn't. Minerva once told her straight out: "I don't trust anybody except for Carl. And I wouldn't trust him, except he makes me."

Why don't you just stay out of my head, Barbara thought, but the TPs fought to get in, just because it bugged her. Barbara shut an imaginary door and locked her thoughts away in an imaginary room, then sat back in her chair and flashed what she hoped was a smug and knowing look. Why give these shitheads the details?

"Aaaaaugh! Too late," Minerva groaned. "She's closed us out, the bitch." There was a slight note of respect in the way she said "bitch."

Barbara smiled. She brought up an image of the three little pigs inside the imaginary room, with the big bad wolf and her classmates outside. She made the wolf piss on Carl.

"Up yours," said Carl. "I'm ditchin' you, bitch." There wasn't any respect in his tone. With that, he left her head. The others followed, even Minerva. Barbara bricked up the outside of the door and settled back in her imaginary room. She stopped thinking about the pigs, but kept the door and the bricks fixed firmly in her mind.

Then, for the first time since Saturday morning, Barbara began to think about Mrs. Rathbone. She'd known about a lot of dank things, not just chemistry. Though chemistry was dank enough.

She had never told Mrs. R how much she liked her. She'd actually liked this teacher as if she was a person. Well, as much as she could like somebody that old. And now Mrs. R was dead.

Entertain us, Barbie thought. She forgot the brick wall. A vision washed over her: a stocky, bearded man in a cheap green suit walking down a corridor, accompanied by a too-thin, too-tall boy in just-pressed clothes. Oh, fuck: the horny chemist from last night.

Minerva caught on and screamed to the others. "Hey! She sees the sub! It's a beard! And he's with some toothpick dweezle wannabe." The other TVs tuned in to Barbara's premonition.

"Wannabe," said Carl. "That's his name now. Juan-na-be. Juan for short." All the dumb toadies laughed. It was too late, but Barbara put up a block anyway. She brought the picture of the boy to a place no one could find. He wasn't a telepath, that much she was sure.

The sub, Mr. Collins, was totally weird. The minute he walked in, everybody could tell he was paranormal, though they couldn't figure out what he did. The telepaths went for broke on it, but couldn't crack him. He sent two of them down to the assistant principal's office. And they went, which was pretty strange in itself. Maybe that's what he did, thought Barbara. Maybe he bent people to his will, in spite of themselves. Maybe that's how he got girlfriends, since he was such a fat old dork.

"Barbara! Earth to Barbara!" said Mr. Collins in a commanding voice.

"Um. Yes, Mr. Collins?" Oops. Keep the brick wall up. Maybe this guy was a TP.

"You gotta stay tuned in, Barbara! Entertain us!" He thought for a moment. "Here's something easy! Separate the leaders from the sheep! Yes or No! Give me an answer: Do the inner electrons of an atom participate in chemical bonding?"

Barbara felt the class waiting for her to respond to the teacher's challenge. Minerva probed her mind just a little, just a poke to get her attention. Carl glared. Barbara knew she could side with the new teacher or side with the class. She looked Mr. Collins right in the eye and said, "They get a little horny now and then, but that's about it."

Mr. Collins called on the new kid, T'Shawn, who answered, "No."

"Lucky guess, Juan," said Carl in a singsong voice.

That's not his name, thought Barbara. I should call him by his real name. Fuck it, she thought, I might as well call myself Barbie and give up. Why fight it? If it sticks, it sticks. That was leadership ability. Good thing everybody didn't have it.

Anyway, it wasn't a guess, everyone knew the answer. Maybe that's what Mr. C meant about separating the leaders from the sheep. She was curious about Juan, but every time she let down the brick wall to glance his way, she saw a fuzzy cloud form around his head, then start to disintegrate. If she continued to look, she would see something she didn't want to know.

"Who wants to tell us about today's reading assignment? Barbara?" He'd already picked up on the fact that she was interested in chemistry. This was not going to do her rep any good.

"I have no idea, Mr. Collins, but Minerva could probably tell you."

Mr. Collins looked at Minerva. "Maureen?" he said.

Minerva recited in a bored voice. "Valence electrons are those electrons farthest from the nucleus, which are responsible for chemical bonding within the atom. I could go on, but I don't really give a fuck."

The rest of the class snickered. Mr. Collins looked confused. Barbara felt a little sorry for him, but then she thought of Mrs. R, dead and everything, and hardened her heart to this grotesque nerd. He didn't even know most of the class could read his mind.

Juan — T'Shawn — spoke out of turn, but politely. "Mr. C, is this your first day of substitute teaching?"

"Nevermind," Mr. Collins answered, smiling broadly. His cheeks puffed up and took on a ruddy tone. His beard somehow looked softer and whiter.

"Hey, it's Santa," said Carl. "Santa C." The suckups snickered again.

Mr. C opened his mouth to speak, then seemed to change his mind. He shook his head and a wave of laughter shook its way up from his gut and burst out of him like the explosion in the sink. "Ho, ho, ho!" boomed Mr. C. "Ho! Ho! Ho!" Mr. C was starting to look scary rather than jolly, though he kept on laughing. Even the telepaths seemed a bit subdued. His beard looked scruffy now, and Barbara noticed that his ears were kind of pointy. Had they been that way before?

"What's so funny?" she asked. Her voice quavered a little. It had been doing that a lot lately.

Mr. C's laughter trailed off; he coughed a little and seemed more like a teacher than he had all morning. "Some of us need to get a handle on the real drama of chemistry," he said. "It's life and death stuff, guys. You've got to take it more seriously. Quiz tomorrow. I strongly recommend that you study sections twelve-nine through twelve-twelve: 'Predicting Redox Reactions.'"

The bell rang, signaling second lunch. Second lunch was noisier than first lunch, and chances of getting physically damaged were somewhat higher than they were in the halls between classes, though certainly not as great as at the bus stop after school. Barbara usually brought a sandwich and ate it on the bench in front of the secretarial station, the safest place on campus.

"Macaroni and cheese, or beans and rice with a choice of condiments," said Minerva, wrinkling her nose. "That's all that's left. They're laughing at us right now in the cafeteria." She eyed Barbara's backpack. "Wish I could see into the future. I would have known to bring my lunch."

Carl rushed to hold the door, watching to make sure no one told Mr. C that the telepaths would know the answers to any test. They'd probe Mr. C's brain like fruit-salad jello, pulling out plump little facts and formulas. The telepaths would, anyway. Barbara and Juan and a few of the others would have to study. She tried to predict her grade, but she just couldn't see it. If he graded on a curve, Barbara knew she'd be in trouble.

"Ace it," whispered Minerva, reading her thoughts. "Look ahead and predict what I'm gonna write on my paper. I bet I'll get an A."

Barbara nodded. "Yeah, you will, but I can't see the test. I can't control when I premote." That's why the government wouldn't give her a scholarship: no military applications, they said. You couldn't count on it, but it thrust itself on you at the worst times.

"So why don't you just copy off my test when I do it? Sit close, and I'll let you see it. It's retro, but it works."

Barbie sighed. She hated having to explain this. "I can't cheat," she said. "I can see the consequences, or something."

"Well, nevermind then," said Minerva, with a toss of her shiny bald head. She stomped away to join Carl and the other telepaths. They walked down the hallway in a group, heading toward the cafeteria.

Barbie walked slowly down the hall in the other direction, toward her locker.

Here's a formula for creating a teenager: take a negative charge, constrain it in time and space, add a catalyst, and get away. Get away, Barbara thought, and she started running down the empty hallway. Faster, she thought. Why not? Even the monitors had gone to lunch.

Then she heard footsteps following her, light as raindrops on a window. Startled, she stopped and turned, twisting her stun ring. She was ready to fight if she had to. It was Juan behind her. He braked to a halt about seven feet away, grinned, and shrugged his shoulders apologetically.

She kept her finger on the stun ring's safety, but she wasn't really afraid of this guy. At least he didn't have pointy ears.

A vision flashed before her — of the principal, Mr. Madonna, nibbling Mr. C's ears. She blinked and it went away. They do that? she thought. Jeeze. The things she didn't want to know about.

"I heard what you said to Maureen," Juan said. He licked the corner of his mouth. "I want you to know I don't cheat either. At least not in any conventional sense of the term."

Barbie started walking down the hall towards him, and towards the cafeteria. She could tell he wasn't going to jack her or anything. He fell in step beside her.

"I'm sorry if what I did last night, like, made it worse for you," he said. "I heard she was a spesh. I wanted to be in her class. When I thought she killed herself, I was really mad at her."

Barbara didn't want to talk about it. "So, who'd *you* kill, to end up at Cobain?" she asked.

"That's rude," said T'Shawn with a slight smile. He shrugged. "The principal at Dick Silly thought I'd be better off with a bunch of other young people who were troubled like myself. For my social development, of course."

Dixie Lee Ray was the academic magnet school sponsored by Microsoft-IBM. There were hardly any speshes there, and certainly no telepaths, who usually developed "behavior problems" by the age of fourteen.

They stopped by Barbara's locker, and she fumbled with the lock and opened it. As she put her chem book inside, T'Shawn held the door and leaned in to give her a kiss. She thought for a second — but only a second. She kissed him back.

When school ended, Barbie walked as slow as she could, trying to look natural, like she wasn't in a hurry. Minerva spotted her and waited.

"Are you okay?" Minerva said. "Don't forget what I told you. About the test? My answers are yours." She seemed hesitant to leave, and the niggling worry that she was about to be busted caught Barbie off guard. Before she could stop herself, she was thinking of Juan.

"Oh," said Minerva. "That's what your problem is."

Barbie shrugged.

"Hey, entertain us," said Minerva. "You've got it bad, don'cha?" She smoothed her bald head and closed her eyes, concentrating. Barbie expected to feel the icy probe, but didn't. "Your pathetic secret is safe with me," Minerva said.

Barbie was embarrassed to face her.

"I'm not gonna tell, don't you get it?" She reached out as if to pat Barbie on the shoulder, but must have thought better of it. "Nevermind," she said with a salute. "See you tomorrow."

The next day, when Mr. C passed out the quiz sheets, Barbara felt ready. Nervous, but ready. "Don't turn them over until I say it's time," he said.

Carl looked at the wall clock. He closed his eyes in mock sleep and murmured smugly, "Wake me five minutes before the bell rings." Barbie wanted to kick him.

Mr. C stood behind the low counter, surrounded by buckets and burners and flasks of labeled chemicals. "Okay now, everyone turn over your sheets. Entertain us!"

Papers rustled like leaves. Minerva giggled. "Prank! A blank!"

"They're all fucking blank," said Carl. He sat up.

Mr. C's face went slack and his eyes rolled back to show the whites. He swayed from side to side and a low rumbling noise came from the area near his mouth.

"Oh gross," said Minerva. "Here it comes — his claim to fame. God, I hope he isn't a contortionist."

"I thought they killed them at birth," said Carl.

"That's abortionists," said Minerva.

"He's not a contortionist," said Juan. "It's something else."

Mr. C opened his eyes, but the expression was glazed and unfocused. His lips moved as if he were chewing something. A low voice came out between them, but the words didn't match the way his lips moved. It was like he was being used as a megaphone by someone inside his head.

"Ticonderogas sharpened and ready?" asked a gentle voice. "It's so good to be back here in the Northwest. Born in Portland, you know. This is a test I always wanted to give my students at Caltech, but unfortunately not a one of them was expendable. Geniuses every one, the little bastards." He cleared his throat. "The test takes the form of a real-life chemistry experiment. I hope you studied hard, because you'll need to stop the reaction before it kills you."

Mr. C seemed to be growing taller and thinner. His neck got longer, his skin grew looser, hanging in wrinkled wattles, like a turkey's.

"Oh my God! He's so incredibly old! Ooh! I can't look," said Minerva, covering her eyes.

"What's happening to Mr. C?" Barbie asked. "Is he gonna die too?"

Carl got that look, like he was probing the teacher. His jaw dropped. All the telepaths listened in.

Minerva whispered to Barbie. "It's not Mr. C," she said. "It's some scientist dude…. Huh! I know who it is! Mr. C is channeling Linus Pauling! Mr. C. can talk to the dead!"

"What," said Barbie. "Who's Linus Pauling?"

"I dunno, he's sort of blank inside, because he's not really here — he's dead. I think he invented vitamin C or something."

Pauling scooped a yellow lump from an unlabeled cannister and transferred it to a burette. "I love this!" he said, clapping his hands. He opened the valve on the bottom of the burette, just enough to let an anorexic stream of powder drip onto the counter. He fiddled with his keys and walked slowly to the door. "Locks from the inside," he said, putting the key in the lock and turning it. "Just in case we want you whippersnappers to stay put." From his pocket he brought out a small bottle and added an eyedropper full of clear liquid to the burette. "Whoa, baby," said Pauling. His eyes glistened.

White gas roiled up and wafted toward them as the students watched in disbelief. By the time the visible cloud reached the front row, the entire class was coughing and rubbing their eyes.

"Augggh!" cried Carl, in tears. "It's concentrated dog fart!"

The odor was pungent and extremely unpleasant. Barbie choked. Carl was wrong: dog farts smelled better.

"Anybody study the material?" Pauling asked. "Hope so, for your sake."

"Hydrogen sulfide?" Barbie asked tentatively. Juan nodded.

"This substance is, of course, extremely unpleasant to

breathe," said Pauling with a chuckle. "And oh yes, it could in fact kill you." He reached into a cardboard box on the floor and pulled out two containers and a rubber gas mask. "We have here two chemicals with which I'm sure you are all quite familiar, as you have just read Chapter Twelve. Each chemical will react in a different way with the element I've just liberated into the air. One should neutralize its effects; one may create a substance even more noxious than the one you're breathing right now." He chuckled.

"Hey-hey. If you're guessing, your odds of staying alive are fifty-fifty. If you studied last night, your chances improve."

His face disappeared beneath the gas mask. Then he jumped up on top of the counter, pulled his shirt-tails out of his pants, and shook his hair down over his face. He bent his knees and played an invisible guitar. A familiar voice echoed from the gas mask, singing. "No one is ever too young to die...."

"This is no time to entertain us," yelled Carl, tossing a half-full can of Pepsi at the Cobain impersonator.

"Mr. C! Don't do this!" screamed Minerva. "It's not fair!"

"Life isn't fair," said the man who looked like Linus Pauling. "You twerps have the attention span of fruit flies. Solve the problem, or you'll have their life expectancy too." He adjusted his gas mask. "This is it. Give me the answer or die trying."

The fumes from the spilled chemical were becoming unbearable. Barbie felt as though her nose was on fire, and her eyes stung. It was the second time in two days that a guy had tried to suffocate her, which kind of pissed her off. Then she noticed that she couldn't actually smell the stuff anymore, though her nose still burned. Maybe it shorted out, she thought. Did noses do that? She was starting to feel sick.

Suddenly, T'Shawn grabbed her wrist, and they both rose to the ceiling. She sucked in a deep lungful of untainted air. The chemistry test, heavier than air, was roiling below. Some of the students were trying to get out, but the door was locked and the windows were barred. "Are they all going to die?" she asked.

"Don't worry," said T'Shawn. He leaned in close to kiss her. "We'll take care of it."

It was exciting to be near him like that, unnoticed and apart from the pandemonium below. She slid her hands around his waist and drew him closer. He put his mouth on her earlobe, and she suddenly understood about ear nibbling: your ears were hotwired to your twat. Electricity spread throughout her body.

They were both breathing hard. He reached up under her shirt.

"Don't," said Barbara. "I mean, there's all these people."

"I don't think they're paying any attention," said T'Shawn. He reached between her legs, and for a moment all she could think about was getting him inside her. His hand, his cock, whatever.

She fumbled with his belt buckle, trying to get it undone.

"We've got time," he said. "We can do it and get out. We've got time."

"I never flunked a chemistry test in my life."

He laughed. The sounds of coughing below grew louder.

"What the fuck," yelled Carl, from the floor. "Anything's better than just standing around with our thumbs up our asses." He reached for a canister, without even bothering to read the label.

"All right!" said T'Shawn. "Acetic acid." He laughed.

"No," said Barbara. "We really have to help them."

"Not yet," he said. "We've got a couple of minutes."

Minerva was choking and sobbing.

"I'm sorry," she said, and let go of him. She took a deep breath, and dropped to the floor. She made her way to the front of the classroom, eyes watering, and found the canisters that Mr. C had set out. Hydrogen peroxide — that would do it. Oxidize the hydrogen sulfide and stop the reaction. She grabbed the H_2O_2 and baptized the burette.

The production of caustic gas stopped, and Mr. C gave her a thumbs up, then unlocked the door and opened the windows. He smiled genially. "Barbara, you did very well, though it took you a bit longer than I expected. A+ for you. Carl, you were about to toss acetic acid into the burette, which would have liberated the hydrogen sulfide more quickly, raising it to lethal levels. I'm afraid you flunked. The rest of you will be graded on the curve. Take five megs of vitamin C and get a good night's sleep away from nuclear fallout. Next time I tell you to study for a quiz, I'll expect better results."

"Way to go, Carl," said Minerva hoarsely.

"Asshole," said Angela. "Class president. Hah. Class turd."

Carl was studying his shoes. He didn't look up.

Friday was the day of the Celebration of Life for Mrs. R. The bus from Cobain Magnet High lumbered through the gates of the cemetery. Inside, Barbara looked at a hillside marked with uneven rows of oddly shaped tombstones. Grey granite plinths, long red chaises-longues like swimming-pool furniture, low cement scrolls with lambs lying on top, Japanese garden lanterns. It wasn't a nice tidy cemetery where all the headstones were set flush with the ground so they didn't get in the way of the lawnmowers. It was a little wild-looking, with weird bits — kind of like Barbara's hair, actually. There were weeds.

A row of huge cement boxes blocked the road beyond the sign. They were maybe eight feet long, four feet square. Not recyclable. These boxes were built to last, and to keep whatever was inside from getting free. Barbara wondered what they were. Then the bus stopped abruptly and the rude truth about cemeteries hit home. Duh.

"He-e-ere we are!" said Mr. Simmons, the death sciences instructor. He got up from his seat and stood in the aisle, facing the special-skills students. Nobody paid any attention to him, except for Barbara, who wished she'd gotten a seat further back with her friends, not that she had any.

Mr. Simmons jangled his key-ring against a bronze plaque that was bolted to the back of the driver's seat. At one time it had read "Sponsored by Microsoft–Boeing," but someone had lasered it to say "Sponsored by Microsoft–Boring."

The class quieted down. "Everybody out for Eternity," said Mr. Simmons cheerfully.

The students dragged themselves out of their seats and fought for standing room in the aisle. Carl was first off the bus, of course. He leaped into the grey November chill and scoped out the terrain.

"Note the cement bunkers to your left as you exit the bus," said Carl. "If anybody starts shooting, get those bunkers between you and the guns as fast as you can."

Barbara wondered if she could project her thoughts to bounce off the sides of the boxes, like billiard balls. Risky, but she thought she could do it. She rounded her thoughts into a ball, smoothed off the clues to who she was, and flung them at an angle between two cement boxes. "They're *tombs*, not bunkers, you sphincter!" She blanked her mind and tried to look nonchalant.

" — sphincter! — sphincter! — sphincter!" Huh. There *was* such a thing as a psychic echo.

Carl whipped his head around, and all the other telepaths snickered. He looked suspiciously at Barbara, but she was doing logarithms in her head. "Buttmunch," he muttered.

Hah. Leadership suck. Nobody was going to shoot at them in the cemetery. Jeez.

Mr. Simmons was talking about some guy who was buried in

the cemetery. "Interesting man, Bruce Lee," he said in a musing tone. "He was an actor and a martial arts expert. Bit of a philosopher, too. Started his own martial arts school...."

"There was a TV show called *Kung Fu*," he continued. "Supposed to be about the spiritual side of Asian martial arts. But Bruce Lee found that there were no acting parts for a Chinese martial artist and philosopher on a show about Chinese martial arts and philosophy. They gave his part to a hippie white guy."

"That guy's buried next to Brandon Lee, that goth actor," said Minerva. "Wonder if they're related."

Mrs. R's grave was towards the back of the cemetery, near the chainlink fence that separated it from the playground at Volunteer Park. It was dark there even in the middle of the day, and it didn't have the great view of the mountains that Brandon Lee had. Kind of where you'd expect to find someone who made a teacher's salary.

There were a lot of people milling about in the cold. All the science classes from Cobain were there, of course, plus some college types who had probably gone to Cobain years before. There were old people she didn't know, and even older people she was sure she'd never even heard of. Mrs. R's family, probably.

A plumpish bearded guy in a dark suit sat on a folding chair near the grave, his head in his hands. He was trembling a little bit; he was crying, Barbie realized. She looked around, feeling helpless. She didn't know guys would cry.

She held her body in a polite position that looked as if she was listening to the service, and set up a double-thick brick wall inside herself. She counted the bricks and got up to two thousand. She looked at the sky, which was astir with dark, bulbous clouds. She glanced around the crowd, and slipped away to its farthest edge. She didn't want to listen to what people were saying about Mrs. R.

The road she was standing on was old, and had sunk a bit into the earth. There was a high curb containing the hillside, and Barbara sat down on its edge. The speakers' voices droned on, trying to make sense of stuff that didn't have to make sense.

At the back of the crowd, Carl stood on a gravestone to get a better view. Other kids followed his lead, of course, and soon there was a whole cluster of them standing there, a meter taller than anyone else.

Barbara cringed. She looked at the tombstones next to her, an odd arrangement of bed-like slabs of polished red granite with cylindrical pillows at their heads. There were two long ones, side by side, and a short one set at a right angle, like camp cots in a small tent.

She read the inscription on the short one's pillow. Regina Mary Dugan. Born 1896, died 1901. A five-year-old child. The others would be her parents, Barbara thought. She read their pillows, to give the family all its names. Mary Frances Dugan, 1845–1883. T. Constantine Dugan, 1874–1901.

So Mary Frances died 13 years before Regina Mary was born. Her grandmother? Poor little kid. Buried next to some grandmother she'd never even met. With her father, probably. He died the same year, so maybe it was an accident that killed them both. Or a fire, and he tried to rescue her. Where was Regina's mother? Remarried? Dead somewhere else, no doubt.

All these tombstones, Barbara thought, and though she tried to push it away, a vision came to her — in flashes, like a slide show. Pictures, click-click-click, each one a different gravesite, with different mourners. Each one a ceremony for someone who had died. Thousands of them. Dead now, dead then, dead to come. All those people left behind, weeping, alone. Their time would come, too. Buried with strangers.

She didn't want to think about it. Box it up, she thought, in one of those cement vaults. Put your feelings aside, keep them in a box where no one can get to them. Even you. Even *you* can't get to them — that's how it works. That's what Minerva does, and Carl. That's the secret of high school. Box yourself in, bottle yourself up. Explode at leisure.

She heard shouts from her classmates. Each student had been given a 1.5-liter bottle of Coke. They shook the bottles, and now they were uncapping them in unison. She was missing her chance to show respect. Shaking her bottle of Coke, she ran to join the others.

Brown foam surged from the crowd of students into the open grave. Kids cheered. A few cried. Barbara was one of them.

She tossed a handful of dirt in after the Coke. "Goodbye," she whispered.

Then it was over.

"Okay, kids, back to the bus," said Mr. Simmons. "Pick up those bottles before you go."

Carl shook his head and dropped crosslegged on the grass. He gestured toward row upon row of graves. "Forget it. What's the point of going to school if you're gonna die?"

"Hey, Carl's flipping!" said Minerva, delighted. "Entertain us!"

"Just tell me why I should bother," said Carl.

"Get a grip or be a slave," said Minerva.

"Please," said Carl. "Shove the motivational crap. Entertain us."

"Okay," said T'Shawn. He waved his Coke bottle and leaped up a good five feet in the air, scissor-kicking his legs at the same time. When he landed, everyone was staring at him. He started screaming, "Here we are now, entertain us, here we are now, entertain us...."

Carl started leaping too, though Barbara could tell that at first he was astonished to find himself in the air. "Here we are now, entertain us, here we are now, entertain us...."

The whole class found themselves bouncing all over the

Lakeview Cemetery, most of them singing, some of them simply yelping in surprise. The other classes, teachers, and funeral attendees stared at first, then began to twitch and bounce a little bit as T'Shawn found the limit of his strength. Slowly he lowered his classmates to earth. He and Carl came down last.

T'Shawn looked at Carl and shrugged. "I don't know what gets into me, but sometimes I feel like I want to teach the world to sing."

"Then it's a good thing this gig wasn't sponsored by Microsoft–Ex-Lax," said Minerva.

"Entertain us," said T'Shawn.

"Nevermind," said Barbara.

The group headed back to the bus. ⸙

Leslie What and I wrote this story about 1997, and tabled it after the Columbine High School murders. It seemed like over-the-top satire when we were writing it, but only a few years later, high-schools had metal-detectors, suicide counselors, and corporate sponsors, and you could actually see Microsoft from Bruce Lee's grave. Reality has put its grimy pawprints all over our Attitude. This is what happens to science fiction writers.

Green Fire

Eileen Gunn, Andy Duncan, Pat Murphy, & Michael Swanwick

| ISAAC

SEPTEMBER, 1943. Nikola Tesla had been dead since January. George Patton had chased the Nazis out of Sicily and was pursuing them up the spine of Italy. Isaac Asimov, age 23, was learning that he was not a particularly good chemist, and probably never would be.

His superiors at the Naval Air Experimental Station hadn't noticed yet, but Isaac knew that when they did, the raises would stop, and his smart mouth would lead him into trouble. Given a choice between saving his career and mouthing off, he'd mouth off every time.

On that day, September 16, Isaac waited almost patiently at the Navy Yard gate, whistling the Major General's Song and counting the rivets on the guard box. Beads of sweat stood on his forehead. His shirt stuck to his back. Philadelphia in the summer was like Brooklyn under water.

I'm very well acquainted, too, with matters mathematical, I understand equations, both the simple and quadratical. 377 rivets. Not an uninteresting number. A Fibonacci number, in fact, and the product of two primes: 13 and 29. *About binomial theorem I'm teeming with a lot o' news, With many cheerful facts about the square of the hypotenuse....*

Heinlein had told him to wait here by the guardhouse, and

Isaac was convinced he had something up his sleeve. Bob had a hair up his *ass*, anyway, since Isaac had signed that petition about not working on Yom Kippur.

"You don't believe in that stuff," Heinlein had complained, trying to bully Isaac into taking his name off the petition. "*You're* not going to temple! If Bernie hadn't come to you with that petition, you wouldn't even have known when Yom Kippur was. Why not take off Christmas with everyone else?"

"So, Bob, you're telling me Christmas is the official holiday for hypocrites like us?"

Heinlein had a hide like an ox. And he was doing everything in his power to get Isaac to work next Monday on Yom Kippur. He'd recruited Isaac for the job at the Navy Yard, and he took a personal interest in turning Isaac into a gung-ho militarist like himself. It was a lost cause.

For my military knowledge, though I'm plucky and adventury, Has only been brought down to the beginning of the century.... A jeep pulled up and Heinlein waved from the passenger seat. "Climb in! You're wasting gas!"

Isaac got in behind him, and the vehicle pulled away. "What's this all about?"

"Don't ask." Heinlein nodded at the driver. "The sailor here's not cleared for that information." The driver didn't blink.

They sped across the Yard to the destroyer berths at the far end. Isaac smiled as the wind evaporated his sweat. An open jeep was considerably pleasanter than walking, and it wasn't an option usually available to shit-job civilians.

Leave it to Heinlein. He had a pencil-thin black mustache and a beautifully tailored suit. He was as suave as you could be without sliding off the face of the earth. And he could get jeeps.

The private dropped them off next to the DE 173, the USS *Eldridge*, a steam-electric ship so new it still had a price tag dangling from the bow. Heinlein gestured toward it and said,

"They're going to do it, Isaac. This is our ship."

"Did I ask for a ship?"

"The Tesla-coil experiment. The Navy agreed to give it a try." Heinlein was pumped plump with excitement.

"You're kidding?! That's a wild goose chase, if ever there was one."

Not three weeks before, sitting around the mess-hall table, he and Heinlein and Sprague de Camp had tossed around a science-fictional scenario for making a ship invisible to detection by radar, which the Germans were rumored to be deploying. Isaac had jokingly suggested creating clutter echoes by running a current through Tesla coils, and got a big laugh from the others. When the hooting died down, though, Sprague looked up from his plate of miserable beef, and said thoughtfully, "You know that might almost work, except —" Several excepts later, they had a plan, which Heinlein submitted the same day. And now the Navy thought it would work? Isaac mugged astonishment.

Heinlein shrugged. "Well, it's not quite what we submitted, but it's close enough that they want us to go along to observe the experiment." They'd reached the gangplank. He motioned Asimov ahead of him. "Climb aboard, Isaac. We're shipping out."

"Shipping out?" Philadelphia was as far as Isaac ever intended to get from Brooklyn. Heinlein had to be joking. "Fuggeddaboudit, as we say in my country. My wife's expecting me for dinner."

"Not any more, she's not. I sent her a telegram: We're on essential war work, top secret, gone two weeks minimum. Unfortunately, you'll be on board ship for the Jewish holidays, so you might as well work them now and get Christmas off, eh?"

Isaac was no longer mugging — he was astonished, as usual,

by Heinlein's total disregard for his feelings. Heinlein hustled him up the gangplank. "Get a move on. Ensign Hopper is waiting to show us around. He'll introduce us to the officers in charge of the experiment."

"Where's Sprague? Can't he go in my place? It was really his idea — he knows a lot more about this kind of stuff than I do. I'm a chemist, for Pete's sake. The only military information I have is about dye markers."

"Sprague's monitoring the experiment from the base. We need you on the ship." They'd reached the top of the gangplank. Heinlein looked around. "Where's that ensign?"

An attractive woman in a WAVE uniform walked up to them. Isaac eyed her appreciatively: trim figure, mass of dark hair, great cheekbones, lovely face. A brunette version, he thought, of Sprague's wife Catherine, who was without a doubt the most beautiful woman he had ever met. Isaac waggled his eyebrows. "Navy life suddenly looks a lot more attractive, Bob." He was joking, of course, but he welcomed any distraction from the panic welling up in his chest.

The WAVE nodded to each of them in an official way. Since they were civilians, she didn't salute. But she conveyed an unmistakable air of Naval authority in the making. "Mr. Heinlein? Mr. Asimov? I'm Ensign Hopper. I'll be in charge of Project Rainbow."

For once in his life, Heinlein's legendary aplomb failed him. "Excuse me, Ensign, but...you're going to be on board the *ship?*" It was an unbreakable rule that the Navy did not allow women to serve on ships.

Ensign Hopper's mouth twisted ironically. "They made me an honorary nurse." Nurses were the exception to the unbreakable rule.

She turned away.

Isaac could hardly contain his laughter. "Well, Bob," he said softly, so their new superior couldn't hear. "I guess we know now what the Navy thinks of our idea. They put an ensign in charge."

He started whistling again. *But still, in matters vegetable, animal, and mineral, I am the very model of a modern Major-General.*

| BOB

After just a few hours at sea, Bob Heinlein had come to realize that Ensign Hopper was, for a military woman, a remarkably unknown quantity.

"Mind your head, sir."

Footsteps echoing, Bob and Asimov clambered down ladders and clattered along passageways and ducked through hatches still gray-gleaming with primer, led by Seaman First Class Kobinski, who looked to Bob all of twelve years old and as fresh as the ship's paint.

"Summoned below decks by an ensign," Asimov said.

"Stow it. The Ensign's in charge of this project. If she says jump, we say 'how high?' This is the Navy, Isaac."

"If I've been drafted, it's news to me."

Bob was happy to follow orders, even from a woman. Even if it brought his tendency toward seasickness to the fore, as had their interrupted assignment to check the insulation of the Tesla coils at the front of the ship.

Bob, in fact, was actively seeking to put himself entirely under someone's command, and he wasn't too particular about whose. He had written more than once to Ernest King, his commander aboard the *Lexington*, now chief of US naval operations. Admiral King knew Bob's lungs were scarred from tuberculosis, but King knew grit, too, and intelligence, and leadership potential. It was only a matter of time: Bob would be back in action again.

In the meantime, it was good to be aboard a fast, state-of-the-art ship. The *Eldridge* was a *Cannon*-class destroyer escort, 1,230 tons, with the new GM twin-shaft diesel-electric drive. Twenty-one knots, easy. Bob had inspected the *Eldridge*'s armament—the big three-inchers jutting proudly upward, the forty-millimeters in their metal pillboxes barnacled to the hull. He wanted to go below, to see the torpedo tubes with the new triple mounting. "Classified," he was told. As if the whole damn cruise weren't classified!

The *Eldridge* would make a fine command. It would carry 200 men at full complement. One commander, one brain, one will— and 200 bodies to effect that will.

"Mind your head, sir."

They went down yet another empty corridor.

For this "unofficial" maiden cruise, which would be entered in no logbook, the ship carried far fewer than its normal complement of crew. Below decks felt like a house freshly built and furnished, then deserted. It was a weird atmosphere—spooky, even.

As a boy in Kansas City, Bob had been drawn to the sea and its mysteries. He'd read the tale of the brigantine *Mary Celeste*, discovered east of the Azores in 1872 with its galley fires still burning, its mess table laid for dinner, its crew and passengers nowhere to be seen. As he'd gotten older, he'd figured there was probably more to the story than the mystery, and he'd become more interested in the discipline of the Navy, in the structure of a command, in the intricacies of making hundreds of sailors function as a single effective force against the sea and against a common enemy. A few people overboard was a minor mystery, but a single powerful ship, functioning cleanly in peace and efficiently in battle, was a major triumph of human society.

His current surroundings had a certain *Mary Celeste* quality about them. But the ambience was not that of a vanished crew, but of a crew that had not yet filled its cabins. The wonder was not of what had happened, but of what was yet to come. Courage, cowardice, the essential business of men discovering the mettle of which they were made.

"Mind your head, sir."

"Belay that, son." This was *not* Bob's first experience inside a ship, after all.

"Ensign Hopper? Here they are, ma'am."

Bob and Asimov stepped over the threshold of a tiny room— what was it, a supply closet? — and, by entering, made it even tinier. Kobinski wisely waited outside. Hopper turned, hands on hips — she was one handsome woman, Bob realized anew — and smiled coldly. Lovely teeth, he thought.

"Are you gentlemen responsible for this?"

She gestured toward the wall of instruments behind her, an ungainly, patched-together, floor-to-ceiling mess of vacuum tubes, wires, capacitors, resistors, switches, gauges. Bob could see the blobby joins where components had been hastily soldered together and welded to the bulkhead.

"I've never seen this equipment before," Asimov said. "Is it part of the experiment?"

"It is *not*. I noticed it just now as I was tracking wires around the ship, double-checking connections. It isn't standard issue for a *Cannon*-class destroyer, I know that."

Bob peered at the jungle of tubes and wires. "Whatever it is, it's up and running. See those needles? They're tracking toward the right, very slowly."

Asimov shouldered alongside. "Hmm, so they are. What are they registering?"

"Dunno. No markings — just calibration lines."

Hopper's eyes were bright and hard as a hawk's. "Two possibilities. One, the higher-ups have added some new wrinkles to your experiment without consulting us. Or two, the Tesla-coil project isn't the only experiment the Navy is conducting aboard this ship."

Asimov was visibly distressed. So much so that he forgot for the moment his overwhelming preoccupation with his own comfort. "But this will interfere with our experiment! How can we tell—"

The lights flickered. There was a distant percussive noise, like a transformer blowing. The vibrations in the deck became jarringly intrusive — no longer the normal low-level trembling of the engines, but a rapid, foot-numbing pulsation. There was an acrid odor, like burning wires.

All the needles on the mysterious gauges twitched to the right.

"Holy cow," Bob said. It wasn't what he had intended to say.

"Someone has switched on the Tesla coils!" Hopper slammed her hand against the bulkhead.

There was a brief, terrible shriek.

Kobinski burst open the door. "What," the sailor asked, his voice breaking, "the fuck was *that?*"

"It sounded like voices," Asimov said.

Bob nodded. "Dozens of voices."

"Cut off," Grace Hopper said, "in mid-scream."

They turned as one and ran down the passageway. Bob was just behind Kobinski, the other two lagging after. He plunged through a hatchway, misjudged the height, and banged his ᐧ head.

"*Damn!*" Bob staggered and clutched his temple.

Asimov and Hopper rounded the corner, almost colliding with him. Bob straightened.

Kobinski was nowhere to be seen.

Nor could he hear the sound of running feet.

Hopper was the first to speak. "Where did he go?"

Bob looked right and left, hoping to see a swinging door, a vibrating ladder, anything that might explain the sailor's disappearance. Nothing. Involuntarily, he thought of the *Mary Celeste*, the ladle in the galley swinging to and fro above the bubbling stew pot. He felt an abrupt nausea, and was suddenly unsure of his footing. He tried to brace himself, failed, and looked down.

Where his feet met the deck, the steel plating was turning misty, uncertain, translucent. Bob's feet were sinking into the deck.

| GRACE

Grace saw Heinlein begin to slip into the mist and shouted "Grab him!" She seized an elbow and Asimov flung his arms around Heinlein's chest and they both pulled. With a hissing sound, Heinlein came free of the grey ooze. All three staggered backward.

Grace stooped to probe with a pencil the gray-green indeterminacy where Heinlein had begun to sink into the floor. She was careful to keep her fingers out of it.

"Bob, are you all right?" Are you all right?" Asimov shouted. He was a milksop, Grace thought. A city boy. A civilian.

Heinlein shouted something back. Grace wasn't listening. All her attention was on the gray-green mist. At first, it had the viscosity of molasses, but in just seconds, it solidified. When she tried to draw back the pencil, it wouldn't budge. She twisted it, trying to leverage it out and it snapped off level with the deck. She stood up thoughtfully.

Asimov was practically in hysterics, and Heinlein was little better. She had to wonder why the Navy had saddled her with these two clowns.

When she had volunteered for this assignment, Grace had known that the proposal submitted by Heinlein and the others was a load of codswallop, gussied up with wishful thinking. But she'd wanted some experience at sea, and it was her only chance. These civilians had been described as "creative thinkers." What that meant, she'd eventually discovered, was that they wrote for the pulp science fiction magazines.

In a bookstore not far from Philadelphia's Reading Terminal Station, she'd spotted Robert Heinlein's name on a paperback. On the book's cover was a futuristic city bisected by a broad trafficway with a rocket ship swooping above. Grace bought the book, and discovered it was a collection of stories.

She read Heinlein's story with interest, pleasantly surprised to discover that it contained neither mad scientists nor tentacled monsters. It was a mathematically intriguing tale about a fellow in California who built a house in the shape of a tesseract. When a quake shook the house, it folded into itself, providing pathways into other dimensions. Far-fetched, but entertaining, she had thought at the time. Impossible, of course. As, of course, it was impossible for a solid steel deck to suddenly evaporate into mist.

She turned to face the two men who specialized in writing about such impossible things. They were still shouting, though the buzzing of the deck had ceased and there was no real need to yell. Asimov was lamenting having ever listened to Heinlein, and Heinlein was ranting about military discipline. She'd teach them a thing or two about military discipline.

"Gentlemen," she said sharply. They looked up, startled. "No need to bellow. Mr. Heinlein, could you describe what you felt when you stepped into that…stuff?"

"A tingling sensation. Like a low level electric shock. Something pushing against me, as if the deck had become elastic. I could feel it pulsing beneath my foot."

"Maybe a high intensity magnetic field," Asimov said. "A

force field generated by a sudden discharge of the Tesla coils, in combination with...."

"With whatever the hell that stuff is," Heinlein continued. "It's possible that...."

She cut them short. "Any number of things are possible at this point. We'll report to the bridge first and speculate later."

Easier said than done. The squawk box was dead; the ship's power was screwed up and the internal phone system wasn't working. She tried the nearby sound-powered phone, the communication system used in combat situations or anytime the ship's power was down. The sailor who picked it up was gasping for breath.

"You gotta help them," he whispered hoarsely. "They're in the walls. I can't get them out. You gotta help."

"Who is this?" she asked sharply. "Pull yourself together. This is Ensign Hopper."

"They're in the walls, Ensign Hopper. You gotta help. Everything's all fucked up."

"Who else is there? Is the Captain there?"

"They're all here, but they're in the walls."

"Stay where you are, sailor. I'll come up and help." She cut the connection. "We're needed on the bridge."

They hurried through the empty passageways, keeping a suspicious eye on the steel ahead, looking for signs of impermanence.

Just below the main deck they found a sailor who hadn't been as fortunate as Heinlein. His body had sunk into the steel. He looked like a man standing in waist-deep water. He was thoroughly dead.

"The deck solidified after the pulse passed," Asimov said weakly.

Heinlein stared down at the body. His voice was flat. "I'm lucky you pulled me out in time."

"That's what the sailor on the bridge meant," Grace said

with a vertiginous touch of unreality. "They're in the walls. The Captain. The others. They're in the walls and he can't get them out."

She shifted her attention from the corpse to the two writers. Both were pale. "We're wasting time." She stepped around the body and climbed out onto the main deck.

There she paused, momentarily disoriented. Where on earth were they? A hazy September sunset was smeared over the land when she had gone down below decks to check the equipment, just four hours after *Eldridge* left the port of Philadelphia, heading south along the coast. By now, it ought to be night.

It was bright daylight. To the west lay, not land, but thunderous storm clouds. There was a smell of ozone in the air. When she reached up to brush back a lock of unruly hair, static electricity crackled against her hand. The air was warm, thick with tropical humidity.

She saw an island just off the port bow, an island with a white sand beach rimmed with palm trees. Heading directly toward them from the island was a sailing ship, a two-masted schooner straight out of an Errol Flynn movie.

"Pirates," Asimov said softly, and she didn't disagree.

Thunder rumbled overhead.

MANDAKUSALA

When she saw the green fire dancing over the ocean, Mandakusala turned the *Bloody Victory* directly toward it. As a warrior and an officer, directly interfaced with the Navy's navigation banks, she knew that this exact spot off Bermuda was a phase point nexus. If a ship equipped to travel between worlds were to appear anywhere, it would be here.

The Southern Matriarch had been waiting for this day a long, long time.

Her mother, standing beside her, whistled as the ship materialized. "Look at all that iron!"

"Obviously a pre-Scarcity culture," Mandakusala said. "Late industrial capitalism, right on the cusp of an information economy."

"They're primitives, then," Ayapasara said slyly. Her mother was too old to hold a command, but she still made a cunning strategist. "And primitives are easily convinced of their own superiority."

Mandakusala caught her thought. Without putting down the glasses, she began issuing orders: "Go aloft and take down the satellite dish. Tell Cook we need a fat roast as soon as she can heat one up. There are two crates of wine down there somewhere —find them! But first, break open that shipment of hibiscus for the Queen Governor's coronation and distribute them among the crew. I want them to have flowers in their hair and garlands around their necks by the time we close with our target."

Puzzled, her mother said, "Flowers in their hair? Why?"

At last she lowered her glasses. "They're all men."

It didn't take long for the crew to catch on to this fact. They were young women all — rough-and-tumble adventurers, hoping for enough prize money to buy their first husbands. And they'd been at sea for weeks.

They crowded the prow, staring at the men, and calling out to them lewdly.

"That one — I want the slutty-looking boy with the long legs."

"Sweet Goddess, I want them all!"

"Stick your tongue out, little redhead, so I can see how long it is."

"Cease that talk!" Mandakusala snapped. "The next woman who speaks out of turn will be flayed alive!"

The crew fell silent. They knew she meant it.

"As you may be aware, the war with the North has been stalemated for the last forty years. No supplies, that's the nub of it. The iron, the coal, the oil — all used up centuries ago! Yet here before us is exactly such a ship as our scientists have told us must someday inevitably come. One with an engine capable of carrying us to other worlds. Rich worlds. Fat and peaceful worlds. You are all warriors. You have all been blooded in the service of the Matriarch. You know how to kill — now I'm counting on you to do something a little more difficult." They hung on her words.

"Smile and wave to the nice boys. Don't frighten the dears. Make them think you're proper gentlewomen, so they'll let us on board."

They were coming in hailing distance now. Mandakusala counted. Thirty men along the rail. Not many for such a large vessel. One of them called out something unintelligible.

"What language is that?" Mandakusala demanded. "Can anyone speak it?"

"It's Ænglish," someone replied. "They speak it in the Cold Isles. I helped burn a village there once."

"Translate."

"They ask where they are, and what we want."

"Tell them welcome to Bermuda. Say I'd like to speak to their commander."

The message was relayed and a figure stepped forward. A woman.

"Why is she all covered up like a man?" her mother asked.

"Perhaps her breasts are deformed. What does it matter?" Mandakusala said peevishly. This woman looked like nobody's fool. "Tell her we request permission to come on board."

Most of the men were leaning over the rail, their eyes bulging out as if they'd never seen women before. They hooted and waved and blew kisses with shocking immodesty. The captain stood apart with two men who must be her advisors. One was short and plump. The other had a thin black mustache. Their eyes bulged too, but there seemed a glimmer of intelligence in them as well.

A crate of wine was set before her and Mandakusala tore open the lid. She tossed a bottle upward to waiting hands. To the translator she said, "Say we wish to entertain them. We have wine for them. And food as well."

The metal ship's men were almost rioting. Their captain was swearing angrily at this lapse of discipline, but they paid her no mind. Her advisors looked uncertain and confused.

She had them. She could feel it.

"Throw down your ladder!" Mandakusala called. She smelled the roast coming up behind her. "Look—we bring you a feast!"

But then, inexplicably, the small round one's eyes widened with horror. He pointed. Others turned to look. Mandakusala turned as well, but there was nothing to see. Only the roast.

But there was nothing strange about the roast. Nothing! It was a plump Northern infant boy, roasted with an apple in its mouth, one of several that had been taken in a raid on a Gulf Coast fortress.

The men were backing away from the rail.

"Grappling hooks! I want grappling hooks and line! Close with that ship!" Mandakusala cried.

But the hooks and lines had been stored below, and by the time they were out, the metal ship was coruscating with green fire. One of her crew threw a line anyway, and screamed as the power flowed down the rope to burn her black from the inside out.

Two great bolts of lightning slammed into the sky, and the ship was gone.

Mandakusala stared at the roast, lying forgotten on the deck. A flesh taboo. Could it be as simple as that? Had she lost everything — power and wealth and eternal glory — simply because these strangers were vegetarians?

Old Ayapasara hobbled up behind her, and coldly said, "Your own command. Forty warriors. And you couldn't take a ship away from a crew of *men!*"

Mandakusala closed her eyes.

Her mother was never going to let her hear the end of this.

| ISAAC

"What did you do?" Isaac asked. "How did you know to do that? Where are we?"

"I don't know where we are. I ordered the engine room mate to apply power to the Tesla coils, removing us from immediate danger. And I knew to do that because I could read their Captain very clearly. I watched how she held herself and when she gave commands. She wasn't a savage, but the commander of a disciplined crew." There was a note of respect in her voice. "Did you notice how swiftly they obeyed her?"

"Well, I —"

But Hopper was speaking to a petty officer: "The Captain and the other officers are missing and must be presumed dead. That makes me the ranking officer. I want all hands on deck immediately. The mission is over. We need to take our bearings, find out how many of us are left, and get this extremely valuable top-secret bucket back to Philadelphia."

"Ensign, do you have any idea where we are and what's happening to us?" Isaac liked to remind people in positions of power of their own ignorance.

"At this point, Mr. Asimov, I'm considering this theory: that an interaction between the current in the coils and some unknown factor or factors is affecting the physical state of the ship, causing a change like a phase transition."

Isaac saw that she was observing him shrewdly; evidently her ability to read minds was not limited to half-naked Amazons. To his excruciating embarrassment, he found himself blushing.

"Do you have any thoughts on that, Mr. Asimov? Ideas are your provenance, I've been told."

"Well, Grace, I'm afraid that the physics is pretty damn difficult, if you'll pardon my French, so —"

"That's *Ensign Hopper* to you, Mr. Asimov!"

Asimov wilted in the heat of that basilisk glare, and hastily said, "Yes, Ensign Hopper."

He didn't apologize, though. He might stand corrected, but he would not apologize. "I agree that what happens to the ship is like a phase transition, when matter changes from being a solid to being a liquid or a gas. Except instead of a transition between different states of matter, this is a transition between matter and time. There's some unknown physical property involved in the way the ship interacts with space and time. It retains its solidity when the current isn't running through it, and sublimates into gray-green gas when it is. We could be in the future or the past or even in some other universe."

"So why do some people get stuck in the walls, when others don't?"

"Um…could be anything. Body chemistry? Rubber shoes? Blood type?"

"Figure it out, Mr. Asimov. It's time you and Mr. Heinlein earned your keep. Because I don't think we're going to just sail back to Philly without some serious brain-cell work."

Isaac asked again, "Where do you think we are?" And where, for that matter, was Heinlein? He had disappeared.

"In one sense, we're pretty much where we've been headed all along. See those clumps of seaweed?" The ocean was festooned with tangles of weed. "Sargassum. We've overshot Bermuda and we're now in the Sargasso Sea. The question is *when* is now?"

Peering over the rail, Isaac saw something moving at the bow. It was Bob Heinlein, the crazy son of a bitch, crawling the huge degaussing cables.

The still, seaweed-filled water ahead of the ship's bow stirred, then churned. Heinlein didn't notice. A huge tentacle lifted from the water and reached for him.

| BOB

He was right! He thought he had glimpsed an extraneous cable from the deck, when everyone else (including, Bob noted with satisfaction, Grace) had eyes only for the Jane Russells on those cannibal women. But he couldn't be sure without going over the rail for a closer look. And here it was, most definitely an extra, smaller cable, no thicker than Bob's arm, twined amid the larger cables, which were plenty large enough for a surefooted and experienced seaman to stand on.

Whoops!

Bob clamped both arms around a cable, as his traitorous right foot dangled in midair. Steady. The footing's slick, but that's no reason to fall. Keep your wits about you. He set his foot back on the cable, tested his weight, took a deep breath of salt spray — and suffered another childish coughing spasm. Damn it! It was like breathing underwater down here, only feet above the waves. But at least the seasickness was kept at bay by the constant wind — the same wind that threatened to sweep Bob off the cables, and into the sea....

Bob pondered his next move. He had to find out where this cable led, and where it came from. Initially he had planned to Jim Hawkins his way completely around the ship, if necessary, but now.... What was that splash? Nothing important, probably. Best to keep his mind on the task at hand.

He heard Asimov calling his name.

Bob froze. He didn't want Asimov or Grace Hopper (especially Grace Hopper) to see him clutching the side of the ship like an overboard cabin boy. Wait a sec! He spied exactly what he was looking for. Now to....

"Look out!"

"Climb, Bob! Climb!"

Something smacked against the hull beside Bob. Foul-smelling ichor spattered his face. He recoiled, nearly falling, and, twisting, saw a tentacle as thick as his torso slithering back into the sea. As he gaped, another tentacle rose dripping from the waves. In the water, something large and gray moved just under the surface.

Falling had been a poor enough option before. Now it was out of the question. So was staying put. Yet Bob couldn't make his limbs move. He watched in horror as the leathery, tulip-like pod at the end of the tentacle waved back and forth at eye level, like the swaying head of a cobra, drooling water, an eyeless predator looking for prey.

"For God's sake, Bob!"

That awful pod lunged for him! Without thinking, Bob turned and ran up the cable. Behind him, the pod splatted against the hull. Grabbing an outstretched hand, Bob pulled himself over the rail and onto the deck, where a small crowd had gathered.

Absently, he wiped his cheek. His palm came away covered with black muck. He cursed and slung it away, over the rails.

Asimov started to laugh, a little nervously. "Bob, I didn't know an old geezer like you could move that fast."

"Stow it, Isaac," Bob said, automatically, but then he began to laugh too. Hopper and the sailors laughed as well, and briefly they all shared the comradeship of danger evaded.

Then the tentacle slapped into the hull again, and Asimov, sobered, said, "I don't suppose that thing can climb?"

"If it could, it would be here by now," Hopper said. "It can't reach as high as the rail."

Bob thought of the smaller ships of an earlier day, those that rode lower in the water, and shuddered. Could the *Mary Celeste*'s crew have been plucked from their ship by just such a kraken? Never mind that: he'd made a discovery that the others should know about. "There's an extra cable. Running amid the degaussing cables." He pointed. "Do you see it?"

They did. "It's like a creeper among larger vines," Asimov said. "Not always visible. How far does it go?"

"It pierces the hull over here," Bob said, grateful he'd spotted the source-location before scrambling for safety.

"Gr— I mean, Ensign Hopper?" Asimov was trying to sound like a sailor. "This cable could be our 'unknown factor' interacting with the Tesla current."

Ensign Hopper looked over the rail. "Right below us is our 'bonus' control room, too. I'm afraid, gentlemen, we've simply come around full circle. We know there's something going on, but we don't know what or who is making it happen."

"We know where the people responsible are operating from, at any rate," Bob offered.

"But they're not here. Maybe they disappeared into a bulkhead during the phase change," Asimov said. "I'd bet my wallet that none of the swabbies left on board know anything. These guy aren't physicists."

The water had grown strangely quiet. Bob pointed it out to the others. "Look at this. The kraken's left, without even a farewell."

They all looked. Where the kraken had been, there was only a kraken-shaped blob of black ink. As they watched, it broke up, dissolved, and disappeared. The brute was definitely gone.

"What do you suppose…?" Bob felt a shadow fall over him.

He looked up to see what had blocked the sun — and saw a glistening gray trunk arching snakelike over the bridge of the *Eldridge*.

Tapering, the trunk rose more than a hundred feet to an impossibly tiny head, flat and flared like the spade of a shovel. It was a plesiosaur, by God! Placidly, like a cow, the critter was chewing something that dangled from its slowly working jaw and, spaghetti-like, inched its way up. There was something familiar about that spaghetti — the tulip-shaped pod at the end. Aha! No wonder the other monster had sped away!

Bob was transfixed again, not by fear this time but awe. Like a rube goggling up at the Empire State Building, Bob looked up, up, up to the apex, the culmination of this strange marine food chain, and thought: What a journey of exploration this could be. The HMS *Beagle* — pah! Think of the wonders, undreamed of by Darwin, that the USS *Eldridge* could bring into port. Think of the knowledge that would flow from it. Think of the stories he'd be able to write.

"My God," Bob murmured to himself. "Sprague de Camp, eat your heart out."

| GRACE

The Sargasso Sea was a convergent zone in the restless Atlantic where warm water and cold came together and changed places, and the action of wind and wave gathered the seaweed and sculpted it into rough circles or long rows. The brownish sargassum, a mass of serrated leaves and little round berries, smelled rank and vegetal, like an exotic soup. Tiny transparent crabs crawled in its tangles.

"...and may God have mercy on their souls," Grace concluded, and the coffins went crashing down through the crabs and seaweed. She smartly returned her hat to her head and, to the assembled crew, said: "Dismissed to stations." They scattered to their tasks with gratifying alacrity.

There weren't many of them left, but it was a good crew. For that matter, it was a good ship and a good command. Only the deaths — the futile and meaningless deaths — of so many trained men, of poor Kobinski and all the others, could dampen Grace's keen appreciation of how fortunate she was to be here.

She made her rounds of the surviving crew, offering a word of praise here, drawing attention to some small deficiency there. The job was to keep the crew crisp and taut as a drumhead — and not a fractional bit tenser. She made sure everybody had work to do, to keep their minds off their strange predicament.

There had been far too many questions about where the ship was and how it had gotten there. She had indicated that their method of travel was top secret, which was true enough. The main secret was that she hadn't a clue how it worked. That was something she needed to remedy.

Heinlein and Asimov were in the closet-sized "secret" control room, picking through the wiring. She left them for last.

Outside the door, she heard Asimov's voice: "Plesiosaurs had a wide distribution throughout the world from the Late Triassic, some 190 million years ago, to the end of the Cretaceous, about 65 million years ago. So that narrows it down to a period of around about 125 million years." From Asimov's tone, Grace could tell that he was quite proud of this bit of useless knowledge.

"What's out there is bigger than any plesiosaur in the fossil record," Heinlein said impatiently.

"That's a good point. The largest of the plesiosaurs was *Elasmosaurus*, which measured in at about 43 feet, about half of which was neck and head. Our friend out there has that beat by around 75 feet."

"So I think we should consider the possibility that we're on an alternate time line," Heinlein said. "It's not just that we're unstuck in time. We are traveling between —"

Grace entered. Asimov was sitting in a corner, back against the wall. Heinlein was smoking his pipe. Neither was looking at the circuits. "Well, you look busy," she said coldly. "I guess you gentlemen must already be done with your analysis of the circuitry."

Heinlein, at least, had the good grace to look embarrassed at being caught gold-bricking. Asimov did not. "We've determined that this stuff is all for monitoring." He tapped the dials that continued their inexorable creep to the right, just slower than human patience could detect. The biggest needle had crept past three notches already — three notches, three jumps? There were a great many more notches on the dial. Hundreds. "The controls are somewhere else."

"And you're sitting here gabbing?"

"Well, I've always been more of the thinker than a man of action," Asimov said.

"Mr. Asimov, how would you like to spend the rest of the war in the brig?"

"I'm a civilian! You have no authority over me."

Grace kept her voice low and even. She had once heard a sailor complain about "getting shrieked at by a squeaky little bitch" after being criticized by a WAVE lieutenant. Since then, she had been careful to avoid sounding shrill, no matter how angry she got. "You're on my ship, Mr. Asimov, a military ship in an emergency situation. There's a war on. I am this ship's only commissioned officer, and I will do what I need to do to make sure my orders are obeyed." She studied him as if he were something particularly unpleasant that she had found on the sole of her shoe. "You are a fool, Mr. Asimov. Don't compound it with insubordination."

Asimov glanced at Heinlein, obviously hoping for support, but Heinlein was standing very straight, his eyes on Grace. He knew how to take a chewing out; she gave him credit for that.

"We were sorting out the possibilities," Asimov said defensively.

"Here are some possibilities," Grace said, her voice icy. "You can obey your orders. You can figure out how to keep us from losing any more men in a phase-shift jump. Or you can spend the rest of the war in the brig. You're far more expendable than a working crew member."

"We're on it now, Ensign Hopper," Heinlein said. "Give us half an hour, and we'll have some answers for you."

"See that you do."

She left.

Back on deck, the Southern boy she had put in charge of the guns said, "We seen half a dozen of those god-damned sea serpents, beg your pardon, ma'am. They was all headed away from us, so we saved us our ammunition."

"Good thinking, sailor."

"Looks like we're in for a storm, ma'am. I smell rain." The sky was dark with storm clouds, and the air was hot and muggy. Grace heard the rumble of distant thunder.

It seemed that everywhere they jumped to, a thunderstorm was brewing. Relevant? She filed it away. "Carry on, sailor," she said, and continued on her rounds.

When next she encountered Asimov and Heinlein, they were busily tracing wires on the bridge. They looked up when she entered.

"Making headway?" she asked.

"Yes, we are, Ensign Hopper," Asimov said. "It's our guess that the phase shifts occur when the Tesla coil causes the ship to vibrate at its resonant frequency."

"You're *guessing*?"

"Extrapolation is a very powerful tool," Asimov said. "Have you ever studied physics, Ensign Hopper? Do you know what the implications are of the ship vibrating in this way?"

"I have some idea." Grace reached for a pencil and a scrap of paper. "At the ship's resonant frequency, we'd get a standing wave. The effect would be strongest at the vibrational anti-nodes." She made a quick sketch, talking while she drew. "When we jump, we all have to stay close to the nodes, the points of least vibration. The anti-nodes are the most dangerous places to be. The bridge was an anti-node, and so was the spot where we found the unfortunate sailor in the deck. Here's a start." She had drawn a rough plan of the ship, with x's at the spots where people had sunk into decks and bulkheads. Asimov was staring at the drawing with a surprised look on his face. "But this is just an effect. It doesn't tell us anything about where we are. What else do we have?"

Now it was Heinlein's turn: "All right, ma'am. You remember that the original plan was to use Tesla coils to create clutter echoes, thus making the ship invisible to radar — only someone made changes to the plan. But suppose those changes were only changes in magnitude? The Tesla coils, after all, merely increase the frequency and magnitude of an alternating current. Suppose the current thus generated was then increased further by another Tesla coil — a Tesla coil the size of a destroyer?

"Once the first Tesla coil was switched on — presumably by the captain, now deceased — the already high-voltage, high-frequency current would feed into the giant 'Tesla-plus' coil" (this was Asimov's ridiculous coinage) "and be oomphed even further."

"Which would explain the massive electrical discharges surrounding each 'jump'," Isaac interjected.

"Are you suggesting," Grace asked, "that if we managed to

reverse the Tesla-plus current, the ship might well jump back-ward — past plesiosaurs and pirates — back to the Philadelphia Navy Yard? How?"

"Well," Asimov said reluctantly, "the Tesla-plus current has to be regulated somehow, but we've checked the bridge, the commander's cabin, the radio room, the engine room, every-where you'd expect to find such a control. Maybe we could —" The shriek of an alarm drowned out his voice. Without hesita-tion, Grace raced for the deck.

| QUETZALCÓATL

Quetzalcóatl came walking across the water, with the storm to his back. His temper was as dark as the storm itself. He had sensed the green fire from a thousand miles away, and transported himself here in a rage. This was his world! He had warned the others not to interfere with it. How *dare* they?

Steam rose up where his feet touched the sea and, because he was drawing power from the sunshine, the air was black around him. Virtual particles scintillated in the blackness like the frac-tured thoughts of a mad god. So terrifying was his aspect that even his beloved plesiosaurs fled from him.

But contrary to his expectations, the source of the green fire was no sleek silver ship from Hy-Atlantis, but a primitive iron behemoth, and its occupants were not of the Evolved People at all but simple anthropoids — humans.

Humans, moreover, from a world where he had once played at creating societies. He remembered well, though it had been long ago, the stone cities and ball courts, the feathered cloaks and tame ocelots, the stepped pyramids he had found thronged with human sacrifices winding slowly toward a peak where the priests waited with obsidian knives, and which he had left cleansed and wholesome. These people had once belonged to him: They had no business here.

Then — outrageous! — the ship's guns began to fire. The fools. Had they no idea how fragile the local ecosystems were?

He had nursed the organisms here through a hundred extinction events, guiding them through the labyrinthine passages of time into forms more graceful and lovely than nature had ever produced on its own.

The intruders must die.

The trick was to do it with a minimum of fuss. He sank down to the floor of the ocean. That would stop them firing any more chemical-powered shells, at least. Then he would plan.

The warm waters closed about him. Ammonites and belemnites jetted swiftly past. Schools of jewel-like teleost fish grazed among the clam reefs.

There were volcanic vents not five miles down. But if he tapped their energies, it would destroy all this beauty. Unthinkable. Better to set up a time gradient and spur the seaweed to hypertrophic growth. That way the ship would be overgrown, engulfed, and dragged under. Or he could....

A distant ammonite caught his eye. Quetzalcóatl swam over to where it rested in the shelter of a rudist clam the size and shape of an oil barrel. When he reached a hand toward it, the timid creature pulled its tentacles into its shell.

"Come on out, little one," he crooned. An apprehensive blue eye stared, blinked, relaxed. "That's right." He extended his hand again.

Slowly, the ammonite unfolded.

It had sixteen tentacles.

Quetzalcóatl held perfectly still, calling to the animal with his mind. By slow degrees it grew used to him. At last it lovingly twined itself around his fingers.

The tentacles were slender beyond belief, a rare genetic doubling, and fully functional. The creature used them with perfect aplomb. Quetzalcóatl peered deep into its genome. Yes! It was stable. The mutation would breed true.

So great was the peace that came over him with this discovery that without even wishing it, he found his thought encompassing the minds of the humans on the ship above. Ordinary enough minds, most of them, both fearful and courageous, and lacking in comprehension, though their commander was extraordinary for her kind. But there were two among them who were peculiar, though no less afraid than the others. Instead of taking battle stations, clutching their weapons and waiting tensely against his return, they were crawling across the deck on their hands and knees, measuring out distances with a length of rope.

Quetzalcóatl plucked language from their minds and listened with interest to what they were saying.

"Fourteen…fifteen…here. This is where your foot started to go through the floor."

"Deck, Isaac. It's called a deck."

"Deck-schmeck, what the heck. What difference does it make? Who's got the chalk? Oh, I guess I do. I'll make a mark."

"Yeah, you'll make a mark all right — as a major fuck-up…."

Quetzalcóatl had heard this sort of banter before, and it did not impress him. Whether they were hunting mastodons or conquering empires, bored and frightened men sounded much alike. He sensed the fear both felt that they'd never reach home. Sensed too the humiliation the younger one felt for being chewed out by his commander, the older one's worry that he was past his physical peak. Both men were coming face to face with their own limitations, and neither much liked it. All this, too, he knew from of old.

What did surprise and intrigue him was that all the while, despite everything else he was saying and feeling, the younger one was thinking about the plesiosaurs. Thinking about their power and beauty, and regretting not having had the nerve to try to touch one. Thinking too of the darkness he had seen coming across the water at them, and feeling outraged that the sailors had fired upon it. Brooding not only on his own fear, but also on the lost opportunities for knowledge.

This was an intellectual honesty out of the ordinary, a restlessness akin to his own. Buried deep as it was under fear and humiliation and anxiety for his future, Quetzalcóatl saw a spark of that same fire of curiosity that burned within his own veins.

"Here's where the cat walked through the wall."

"Bulkhead."

"Whatever. Who's got the chalk?"

Quetzalcóatl released the ammonite. Then he summoned an archelon and rose to the surface, standing on its back.

The ship's crew gathered at the rail at Grace's command. Quetzalcóatl had seized control of her mind, of course. It was easiest to be direct when dealing with primates. Through her eyes he saw himself: tall, auburn-skinned and muscular, with a forbidding expression on his face. It was much the same appearance he had worn when he was worshiped as a god in their own world. Except for the extra arms, the talons, and the jagged horns that swept up from the sides of his head.

In a voice like thunder he said, "Have the young one stand forward."

The young one turned green. He looked helplessly at his friend, his commander, his shipmates, silently pleading for their help. They all stood stone-faced and emotionless. He had no way of knowing that they were not under their own control.

Finally, because he had no choice, the young one climbed

down the rope ladder to the ocean's surface. Hesitantly, he stepped onto the back of the giant sea turtle.

The young one flinched when Quetzalcóatl placed a clawed hand on his shoulder. The terror that thrilled through him was a palpable thing. There were tears of fright in his eyes. But, probing, Quetzalcóatl saw that — yes — there was under all that emotion, a glint of wonder.

Quetzalcóatl smiled to himself. He wished he could keep this one here, to nurture and encourage it. But he was a naturalist. He would create a bubble of air about them and command the archelon to carry them below. He would show this one a few of his choicer treasures. And then, gently, regretfully, he would remove his hand, and release the specimen back to its natural habitat.

| ISAAC

Isaac stood on the leathery back of the giant sea turtle. It swam at a majestic pace through the calm water. A mantle of moss billowed out in its wake, attached to the edge of the shell like the train of a great green wedding-dress. Close to the ocean surface, with the air humid and the hot sun on him, Isaac felt that the boundaries between himself and this strange natural world were not clearly enough defined. He preferred pavement, frankly.

All around him sported plesiosaurs, oddly graceful in the water, like huge penguins with giraffe-long necks, moving their stubby flippers like rudimentary wings. He was unafraid of them, despite their sharp teeth. Somehow fear had lost its context in the light of recent events. Fear was the air he breathed now, and no one thing was more fearsome than any other.

Except perhaps the memory of the obsidian claws of Kukulcan gripping his shoulder. Gukumatz, Nine Wind, One Reed. Quetzalcóatl. Interesting to think that he, Isaac, had encountered someone who was worshiped as a god. He could see how such a situation might come about. Quetzalcóatl certainly gave the impression of being an indestructible entity with unlimited power, all-encompassing knowledge, a life span measured in eons — and wasn't that what a god was?

So why did Isaac not worship him? Isn't that all a god asks, and isn't it right that he ask it? But there was something in Isaac that kept him from giving over the portion of himself that religious people offer as a gift to their gods. He just couldn't do it. He could acknowledge the power, but he couldn't offer obeisance. Perhaps if he worshiped properly, Quetzalcóatl would return him home. Perhaps not. It didn't matter — it wasn't in Isaac to do it.

The turtle was approaching the boat. Isaac could hear the excited yells of the crew, pleased and surprised to see him coming back from what they must have thought was certain death. He waved jauntily.

Bob Heinlein's voice cut through the others. "Grab the ladder, Isaac! It's going for you!"

Isaac looked over his shoulder. Sure enough, one of the plesiosaurs was casually swimming his way. This was his chance to touch it. He had to know what it felt like. Armor-plated? Warm-blooded? He had to know.

He seized the ladder, pulling himself off the back of the turtle. Hooking an elbow around a rung, he leaned outward, as the huge reptile approached, and extended his free hand. The ladder jerked spasmodically and he felt himself being pulled out of reach. The plesiosaur stretched its tiny head up toward him, like a cat wanting to be petted. He was still straining to reach it when they hauled him onto the deck.

The sailors seemed to think he had cracked under the stress of whatever had happened to him below the sea. "You'll be all right, buddy!" one of them kept saying in a tight voice. "You're okay now! You're on the ship, it's okay!" Maybe he was talking to himself.

Heinlein clapped a hand on his shoulder. "Good work, Isaac! What did you find out?" That's Bob all over, Isaac thought. "Good work" meant "I thought you were a goner there." The clap on the shoulder meant "I *really* thought you were a goner." And "What did you find out?" meant "Let's not think about this any more."

"What happened out there, Isaac?" Grace Hopper looked as though she knew more than she was letting on.

"That's 'Mr. Asimov,' isn't it, Ensign Hopper?" Isaac grinned.

"I can see the experience didn't change you much," she said dryly. "Who was your friend, the huge golden hypnotist? I'm not accustomed to being driven like an automobile." It dawned on Isaac that Hopper's experience with Quetzalcóatl might have been even more disturbing than his own.

"He's a retired god," said Isaac, matter-of-factly. "He bred the plesiosaurs — this world is his ranch, I think." He furrowed his brow. "Oh, wait! I know where we are!"

"Just a moment. If the immediate crisis is past, it's time to resume normal operations." She turned to the crewmen, now reduced to about fifty men. "Return to your stations, men." They dispersed, and she turned back to Isaac and Bob.

"I prefer not to have an audience for this conversation," she said quietly. "Continue, Mr. Asimov. Where are we?"

"We're exactly where we seem to be, in the Sargasso Sea." Isaac paused for effect. He couldn't help himself. "But we're rotated through other dimensions than those we're accustomed to."

Hopper didn't seem surprised by the notion. "That's a bit of a stretch from the data at hand. Why do you think so?" Bob, of course, was already nodding. That was the advantage of being a science fiction writer — nothing was ever too strange.

"Quetzalcóatl told me." The information had been poured into him, really, like water filling a pitcher. The ship, with everyone on board, was rotating out of alignment with their familiar dimensions into synchronization with ones they couldn't ordinarily perceive, and each of the phase-change events that they had gone through had rotated them further from the familiar. "And you were *told* this?"

Now that Isaac thought about it, he wasn't so sure that words were exchanged. "He made it clear to me, anyway."

Heinlein was looking at him oddly. "What makes you think it's true?"

Isaac shrugged. "Would a god lie?" Then, "Unfortunately, he didn't say how to stop the process — so I guess we're as far from home as ever, unless the skipper here knows something I don't."

Grace Hopper's eyes narrowed. "Let me see if I can steer you in the right direction, Mr. Asimov." Oops, he thought. "We started off in a space-time continuum that may have an infinite number of dimensional vectors, of which we can perceive four — height, depth, width, and time. Somehow, when we discharge the Tesla coils, the ship rotates relative to these infinite dimensions, and we perceive what's going on in dimensions we don't usually have to deal with."

Asimov knew that Hopper knew something about physics, but non-linear abstract geometry? Who was this woman, anyway? "I apologize, ma'am. But how come it doesn't look any different? Except for the plesiosaurs, and so forth."

"Quetzalcóatl is a pretty big so-forth, but that's a good question, Mr. Asimov. This is just a guess, but it could be that so far, at least, the physics is basically the same, and it's relatively easy to orient ourselves. It might be that if we get knocked out of alignment with all our familiar dimensions, we would find the situation much more disorienting. We've still got one foot on the dock, but we're slipping away."

"I'm not sure I follow you there." Isaac had trouble admitting ignorance, but if anything mattered, getting this right mattered. This dimensional stuff wasn't his strong point.

Bob Heinlein was leagues ahead of him. "That's it, I think, ma'am, the alignment. Isaac, imagine living in only three dimensions — you don't perceive depth, say. Things seem two-dimensional to you, as if you lived on a piece of paper. That doesn't mean the other dimensions aren't there, but so as far as you're concerned, they might as well not be. Now suppose you rotate, so you do perceive depth. Because you live in only three dimensions, you'd lose the ability to perceive one of the other ones — height or width or time, see? You'd still be limited to three. But the other one would still be there."

Isaac could see that. He nodded.

"Now suppose there are more dimensions than three or four. Suppose we inherently four-dimensional beings got realigned with another dimension somehow. We'd lose alignment with one of the ones we've got. Maybe what's happening when we go through these phase-transitions is the dimensional axes are rotated, so that we're no longer perfectly aligned with our familiar world. We're still there, but we can't get at it!"

"Therefore, to get home, we have to rotate our ship back into alignment with the dimensions we want to live in," Hopper said.

"And soon," added Isaac.

"But don't you think it would be *interesting* to try a few more realignments first?" There actually was a pleading tone to

Heinlein's voice. He honestly wanted to take a few more spins through the circles of Hell.

Asimov shuddered. "I don't think—"

A jarring percussive clatter rattled the deck. The entire ship vibrated at a bone-numbing frequency. The area between the lines that Heinlein and Isaac had marked on the deck sublimated into gray-green fog, and the smell of ozone filled Isaac's nostrils. Green fire played over the deck, over the guns, over the conning tower. The fire moved beyond mere green: it was the color of chartreuse tinted with the music of flutes and the vinegar taste of radio waves. It was a color that smelled like butyl mercaptan.

Someone had switched on the Tesla coils again.

"Your wish has been granted, Bob," said Isaac, through paralyzing fear.

| BOB

Wherever they were this time, the weather was awful. Lightning crackled about the masts, waves of thunder boomed, wind threatened to blow everyone over the rails, and rain sheeted down, drenching the three of them even as they flailed across the deck, trying to avoid the smoking zones of green fire.

A wave surged over the railing to port, and foam sluiced past their ankles. Isaac yelled over the roar of the storm: "The chalk marks!" The water was washing them away.

It was too late, in any case. Whoever had thrown the switch had caught many of the sailors unawares, out of position. Ahead, three crewmen dropped, screaming, into the mist, as if through a trap door, and disappeared. Two others, pinned to the starboard rail by writhing, advancing ropes of green fire, leapt yelling over the side. Someone else screamed to port — "No!

No! No!" — and as Bob turned to look, a running man slammed into him, so hard that Bob could feel the man's hot, panicked breath. Bob fell backward, grabbed the railing of a ladder to right himself, and gaped when he realized there was no running man — just a disembodied series of *No*'s above a line of splashes across the standing water on the deck, like those made by a man running straight for the rail. The last *No* turned into a shriek, and the last little fountain of spray subsided as the shriek faded into the wind.

He tripped on something that gave slightly, and looked down to see a dead man's yawning head sticking out of the deck, the lower jaw fused with the steel. Bob had kicked the corpse in the teeth.

"Dear God," Bob said, and for the first time in his life, meant it as a form of address.

Then the green fire was subsiding — and so were the winds, waves, and lightning, Bob was glad to see, though the downpour showed no sign of letup.

The rain washed down over the scene of senseless, senseless death. Bob thought of friends of his who had died at Pearl Harbor, perhaps without even knowing what had happened to them. Did this death have less meaning? Was combat against a human foe morally greater than combat against the cold equations, as Campbell termed them, of physics? He'd wanted to do his part in a just war, but justice had no meaning here.

Here there was no justice, no right or wrong. But wait. He'd forgotten the one element that smacked of Axis sabotage: the supposedly classified torpedo tubes, to which he'd been denied access at the beginning of the voyage. Which lay directly below the mysterious monitoring room.

He didn't go looking for the others. He was a Navy man, after all. He would check this out himself.

"Don't touch that dial," said a strangely distorted voice.

Bob spun around from the control panel, in a crouch, ready for anything.

On the other side of the small room was the image of a little old man with a moustache. It flickered like an old movie, not flat against a bulkhead as a projection should, but in the middle of the floor. It was three-dimensional, sepia-toned. It moved jerkily, as if the flickering concealed movement that the eye couldn't quite follow. It spoke again:

"Don't touch it. The experiment has yet to run its course." The voice sounded far away and staticky, like a storm-ravaged radio signal.

"Who authorized you to be here?" Bob demanded. It wasn't much, but it was better than "Who are you?" or "Damn! You scared the juice out of me, Pops."

The old man smiled. Something about him was vaguely familiar. "It's my experiment," he said. "My coils. My generator. My wireless transmission system. My genius."

Bob blinked. He remembered that face.

The old man gave a courtly Old World bow. "Nikola Tesla, at your service."

"But you died," Bob said. "Back in January. I read about it in the *Philadelphia Bulletin*. St. John the Divine was packed with Nobel laureates. It was quite a funeral."

"What is death? The Mahat, or Ishvara, continues. Throughout space there is energy, the Akasha, acted upon by the life-giving Prana or creative force." His voice hardened. "Step away from that panel." Tesla gestured, and Bob saw that his right arm was wrapped in wire, as a caduceus is wrapped in snakes. The end of the wire vanished in the floor, at the edge of the sepia light.

Suddenly more angry than bewildered, Bob said, "You can't stop me. You're not really here. You're just a projection."

"More like a broadcast," Tesla said. "I'll happily share the details with you, if you like. But for now, come away from those controls."

Bob did take a couple of steps toward Tesla, unwittingly, in his excitement.

"It was you. You're the one who's been meddling with our experiment."

"I improved the experiment, my military colleagues and I." Tesla sighed raspily. "Ah! How good it was, finally to have friends in high places. You didn't go far enough, you know. Using my coils merely to shield a ship from radar! How could you fail to see that the same technology could be used to teleport a ship and its crew almost infinite distances in an eyeblink?"

Tesla added, not unkindly: "But you see, your project served its purpose. It provided us a ship and an admirable cover to put my theories into secret operation. So everything is going according to plan."

"Are you mad?" Bob retorted. "Can you actually see what's going on aboard this ship, from — wherever you are? We'll be lucky if any of us get out alive. Listen." He felt he was arguing not with a ghost, but with less than a ghost — a notion, a memory, a dream. "I'm a fiction writer. A couple of years ago, I wrote a story about an architect who designs an inter-dimensional...."

"Yes, I read that one."

Bob momentarily forgot his anger. "You *did?*"

"I read all the Gernsback magazines." Tesla lifted his coil-wrapped arm in a gesture that might have been wistful if not for the stroboscopic effect, which reduced it to a visual stutter. "I found it an entertaining conceit. Though it was of course more a lecture than a story. With some trick effects at the end."

Bob flushed, but plowed on. "Then you know what I'm talking about. The effect is uncontrollable. The architect and his friends barely make it out of the house with their lives. That's what's happening here on the *Eldridge*, Dr. Tesla. We're not jumping through three-dimensional space, we're jumping across the dimensions themselves."

"A simple malfunction, easily corrected once you return to port."

"How do we get back? How do we terminate the experiment?"

Tesla winked out of existence, leaving Bob dazed and blinking at a bulkhead, as if he had been staring, eyes burning, into a light bulb at the moment it was switched off. Then Tesla was at his elbow. Bob yelped. Close up, Tesla's face was grainier, like the front-row view of the bottom edge of a movie screen.

"How can you give up now?" Tesla asked. "As the jumps come faster and faster, you won't even register their passage. All possible worlds will cycle past you, faster and faster, until all realities are experienced simultaneously."

Through Tesla's glowing face, Bob could discern the faint lines of the instrument board. "But how will we get home? How will we stop?"

With a pop of static, Tesla winked. The effect was not comforting, as the eyelid stayed down just a half-second too long. "Who cares? Think of the glory!" The old man was no longer looking at Bob, but lost in his own reverie. "Only by annihilating distance," he murmured, "can humans ever end the scourge of war. Imagine! Instantaneous transport — all men neighbors! No more war!"

Nikola Tesla — whether dead or alive, real or not — was mad as a hatter. Bob realized that the time for talk was over. It was time for action.

Bob leaped for the control panel he had been warned away from. There was a joystick there, mated to a potentiometer. It was calibrated from a central point with positive and negative numbers, and the pointer was set to the extreme left. He slammed it all the way to the right.

Tesla snapped out of existence, leaving only a lingering aftereffect on Bob's strained eyeballs, and a faint acrid odor, like a carbide lamp.

The now-familiar rumbling started again.

| GRACE

From a raging storm, the ship had been transported to a sea that was as still as glass. The sky was dark but it slowly filled with millions of twinkling mothlike creatures the shape and texture of doilies, and the size of delicate clumps of snowflakes. They glowed faintly. But they seemed to be harmless, though their trilling was threatening to get on Grace's nerves.

Grace stood on deck, watching the snowflakes swirl. It was night here, wherever "here" was. By ship's time, it was also night. Grace had set a watch and ordered all sailors not on watch to their bunks. Everyone was tired, and tired men made mistakes. She herself was weary to the bone. How long had it been since she had stopped to rest or had grabbed a bite to eat? She had volunteered for this assignment so eagerly! All she had wanted was a bit of experience at sea, all but impossible for a woman to get. And now she had a command.

The moon was almost full. Overhead, the snowflakes spun in the moonlight. Tiny flying flecks of lace, each about as big across as the tip of her little finger. A few of them landed on the deck, and she examined them. Each had a unique pattern on its lacy wings. Like snowflakes, maybe — no two alike.

Idly, she held out her hand and watched as a snowflake landed on it. Its tiny feet tickled her palm. Its wings, extended, formed a lacy circle around a tiny body no bigger than the head of a pin. As she was watching it, a snowflake landed on her other hand. She was idly studying the newcomer when two snowflakes that were somehow joined together fluttered past, just in front of her eyes. Were they mating?

Now there as a minuscule tickle on her right hand. Another snowflake had landed near the first. Then a chain of three snow-flakes fluttered past her eyes. Startled, she stepped back, lifting the hand that held the snowflakes.

Two more snowflakes landed on her left hand, making three on that hand and two on the right. A chain of five circled her. She shook her head, astonished.

"Wherever we are, it's an improvement." It was Asimov, returning to the deck. "What are all these flying whatchama-callums?"

"They're insects of some kind." She laughed. "I think they are trying to teach me arithmetic."

The snowflakes regrouped and tried something different. Two went by, then two more, followed by four. Three and two were followed by six, four and two by eight. "Multiplication," she acknowledged. She flashed five fingers two times.

They regrouped again. Four came by, followed by two groups of two. Nine, followed by two groups of three. Sixteen, followed by two groups of four. "Square roots!" she said. She flashed five fingers five times with her left hand, then flashed five fingers twice with her right.

A third regrouping. Grace was expecting cube roots. Instead, the snowflakes glided by slowly in a long line: a flake, a space, a flake, a space, two flakes, a space, three flakes, a space, five flakes, a space, eight flakes, a space, thirteen flakes, a space....

"The Fibonacci sequence!" Asimov couldn't keep his mouth shut.

"They're talking to *me*," Grace complained jokingly, and flashed twenty-one fingers.

Asimov held out his hands. A snowflake landed on each, starting him out simply with one plus one.

"No short cuts," said Grace.

"Perhaps they form some kind of collective intelligence," Asimov mused. "The whole is more than the sum of the parts. That's the theory behind computers, after all. Each relay is a binary decision point. But put them all together and...." He waved his hands. The snowflakes were up to three plus two: three on his left hand; two on his right.

Asimov was being patronizing again. But watching the snowflakes had mellowed Grace's mood. "I know all that already. If we make it home," she said, then corrected herself: "*When* we make it home, I'll be working with the Mark I." The Mark I was the world's first large-scale automatically sequenced digital computer.

"Oh," Asimov said humbly. "I should have figured. I'm always attracted to beautiful older women who are smarter than I am."

"Isaac, if you were a military man, that would be insubordination. But I'll overlook it in a civilian," Grace said absently. She addressed the snowflakes politely. "What I need to know is how to find our way home. Simple arithmetic won't help me there. It's more of a geometry problem."

All the snowflakes formed a whirling ball in the air. Individual flakes flew out, one, one, two, three, five, eight..., the smaller groups converging loosely in a dome over Grace and Isaac, who for once stood speechless. The dome grew quickly until it contained hundreds of the insects, arranged in helical spirals like the seeds on a sunflower. Responding to invisible cues, they whirled in place, first to emphasize their arrangement in left-twisting spirals, then to emphasize their right-twisting spirals.

"I have no idea how to respond," Grace said to Isaac. "I don't know what answer they want from me on this one."

As they watched, six snowflakes, along a single helix winding down from the top, started whirling madly, then curved in on one another in a small loop back to the top.

There was a message there for her, she was sure, but she

couldn't figure it out.

Grace felt something in the air — a crackle of static electricity. "Wait!" she cried, but the ship's vibration drowned out her voice. St. Elmo's fire crackled among the guy cables and railings. They were jumping again.

She closed her eyes, striving to retain the image of the snowflake sphere, with its helices and loop. Suddenly the air on her face was cold. The breeze carried a chemical taint that reminded Grace of drying paint and diesel exhaust. Her breath burned in her throat.

She opened her eyes. The snowflakes were gone. The moon was gone. The sun was low on the western horizon, setting cold and red over dark, still waters.

In her heart, she mourned the loss of all the snowflakes were about to teach her. Now she knew how it must have felt to an Alexandrian scholar to stand watching as the Great Library burned.

The vibrations shuddered to a stop. Duty called. Putting away all thought of the snowflakes, she asked, "Where are we?"

"At the end of the world," Asimov murmured, his face bleak.

They found Heinlein on the main deck pushing through a crowd of sailors roused from sleep by the jump. The sailors clustered at the rail, staring at the dim sun that hung motionless over the black water. There was no life in that water; Grace knew that. And somehow, that absence of life was more threatening than any number of krakens and plesiosaurs.

Heinlein wore an expression that combined mortification and despair. Grace knew in a glance that he had been responsible for their last jump. "You pulled the switch," she said. "Where was it?"

"I didn't have a choi—" He caught himself. "In the torpedo room."

"You acted without consulting your commanding officer? You simply *acted* on whatever thought came into your head?" He had ruined their best chance of getting back now. "No wonder you were refused a commission, Mr. Heinlein. You are not cut out to be part of a military force."

He looked as if she had spit in his face. "It seemed important to act, Ensign Hopper. There are…forces conspiring to keep us from getting home. So I set the controls for full reverse."

"It was an honest mistake." He was, she suspected, cracking under the stress — and how long before that happened to all of them? She had to help Heinlein keep his courage up. Blaming him at this juncture would not help. "But you were acting on the misconception that we were operating in a linear system — switch it one way, we go forward; switch it the other, we go back. Clearly, it's not that simple." Asimov stood at the rail, as if mesmerized by the setting sun. She turned away from Heinlein to give him time to collect himself. "Talk to me, Mr. Asimov."

He blinked, as if waking from a dream. "Eh?"

"We need to approach this problem from a new angle. The snowflakes were trying to show me something, but…I'm not quite there. Just talk about it. Talk about what we know so far. Explain it to me."

"What we know? We don't really know anything, but we think that resonant frequencies have something to do with it." He started slowly, then gathered speed as he warmed to his topic. "We think that we're rotating through dimensions beyond the four that we normally sense. We're rotating and we need to rotate back into alignment with the dimensions where we live."

"Rotating…," Grace muttered. "And we need to rotate back. If we were rotating in three dimensions, I'd approach this with spherical trigonometry. But we're rotating through a multi-dimensional sphere. Perhaps that's what the snowflakes were driving at. To calculate the length of a jump, we need to consider a projection of that multidimensional sphere into three dimensional space. What are our known variables?"

Heinlein frowned, struggling to answer. "We jumped in space — from four hours south of Philadelphia to Bermuda. Then to the Sargasso Sea. But who knows after that?"

"Distance," she mused. "That's a variable. But how far?"

Isaac, paying attention now, gave her the distances. She pulled a notepad from her skirt pocket and jotted them down. The man really was a fount of trivial information.

"What other variables have we got?"

"Time," Heinlein said. "Time between jumps. If we are looking at the coordinates in multi-dimensional space-time…."

"How long did we have between jumps?"

"We were in Bermuda for about an hour," Asimov said.

"And how long were we with the plesiosaurs?"

"About four hours," Heinlein said.

"We were in the rainstorm for less than an hour, and among the snowflakes for about eight hours," Grace said. "Let me see what I can do with this. Bob, why don't you and Isaac devise a plan for shutting down the generators immediately upon our arrival home. I will assign as many crew members as you need to make it instantaneous." She spoke with more confidence than she felt. "Meet me back here when you're done."

Was it an hour later? Or a day? She didn't know. Someone shook her shoulder and there was Bob Heinlein, looking worried. She had fallen asleep sitting on the deck, doing calculations by the lurid light of the permanently setting sun.

This was a world that had never known life, and never would. She shivered. No matter where they ended up, she wouldn't want to stay here.

By the light of an incandescent bulb, she double-checked her figures. The results of her calculations gave the coordinates from which they had to jump and the time at which they had to discharge the coils. "What time is it?" she said in a panic. "How long have we been here?"

"Four hours," Asimov said.

"Good. Here's what we need to do."

They had four more hours to get to the proper location. Full speed ahead, through the lifeless sea. It was good to rouse the men to power the ship; good to be moving. They reached the jump-off point with twenty minutes to spare.

She was waiting, hand on the switch and eye on the clock, when there was a polite knock on the door. At her command, the last person on earth she expected to see entered, and saluted. "Seaman Kobinski, reporting for duty, ma'am."

"Kobinski?! Where the hell have you been?"

"Invisible, ma'am. I kind of blacked out and when I came to, I couldn't see myself, so I thought, well, maybe I should be in the sick bay." He grinned shyly. "I'm better now."

The second hand swung round to zero-second. "Hang on to your hat," she said, and, praying her calculations were right, threw the switch.

| SPRAGUE

Sprague was sitting in a dim corner of Pop-Pop's Tavern waiting for Catherine when the invisible sailors poured in, looking for a fight.

The irony was that Pop-Pop's was a respectable tappie. It wasn't one of Heinlein's dives, with B-girls hustling two-dollar ginger ale cocktails or a "Magic Window" over the bar where naked women enacted supposedly classical tableaux. Pop-Pop's was the kind of place where the old neighborhood women had their own entrance and a back room where they could buy a quart of beer to drink with their girlfriends without suffering the unwanted presence of men.

But it was near the Yard and so there were sailors in the front room. And, being sailors, when challenged they fought back. That their opponents were invisible made surprisingly little difference to the dynamics of the fight. Somebody was jostled when the newcomers rushed to the bar. He threw a punch. It hit the wrong person. The bar erupted.

Sprague saw a sailor lifted struggling into the air by unseen hands. Somebody smashed a chair over his invisible opponent, and the sailor fell to the floor. With a roar of rage, a bottle swooped up from the bar and smashed over the chair-wielder's head.

Sprague was a lieutenant, bucking for lieutenant commander. His first impulse was to break up the fight. He was pretty sure he could do it. Military discipline was all theater, really. A commanding voice and a dramatic presence could quell the rowdiest enlisted man. He had both of those.

But in the time it took to lay down a quarter to pay for his unfinished beer, stand, and tuck his cap under his arm, a better thought came to him.

So, quietly, Sprague slipped into the back room and, with a nod and a wink to its denizens, ducked out the Ladies' Entrance. He didn't want to get involved in an incident that would tie him up for hours with the Shore Patrol. Not now.

He arrived at the sidewalk out front just as one of the invisible seamen pushed through the door, dragging an unconscious sailor by the feet behind him.

This Sprague could not ignore.

In the bright sunlight, the seaman was not entirely invisible — more like a clear glass filled with water, which an observant man could see if he looked closely. Sprague stepped forward and tapped him on the shoulder. He felt solid enough.

The man dropped his burden, spun about, and aimed a haymaker at Sprague's jaw.

Deftly, Sprague stepped aside from the blow. As the fist whistled past, he seized the man's wrist, and twisted — a technique he had learned from a Kuomintang ensign — forcing the fellow to bend over. Then he drove his knee into the man's stomach. Hard.

The transparent ruffian fell to the ground with a concrete thud.

I've seen action at last, Sprague thought. Now, nobody can say I spent *all* the war behind a desk. If only Catherine had been here to see it, though!

"Sprague, what on Earth is going on?" Catherine had come up behind him. "Are you all right?"

Thank you, God.

Catherine stared down at the unconscious sailor. He was slowly fading back into visibility.

"What's going on here? What on Earth does it mean?" she asked wonderingly.

Sprague grinned. His brain had been operating at top speed since this incident began, combining disparate elements, putting together hints and rumors and troubling snatches of radio transmission that had been recorded, shown to him, and then stamped TOP SECRET and filed away forever. Now it processed all the information and spat out an answer: "It means Bob and Isaac are back!"

A couple of days later, Sprague dropped by Asimov's office to find him fiddling with a radio. He had the Bakelite cover off and the innards all over his desk and was inexpertly making connections between vacuum tubes. It looked a terrible mess.

Sprague swept a corner of the desk clear and perched elegantly upon it. "I just ran into Bob in the hall," he said. "I don't believe I've ever seen him so angry."

Without looking up from his work, Asimov said, "It's the report Ensign Hopper submitted to the Navy. You know how when you've got a SNAFU, you put a good face on it by subtitling the report 'Lessons Learned', but when it's FUBAR, you use 'Early Lessons Learned'?"

"I hadn't, but I'm always glad to learn the local lingo." He picked up the report. " 'Project Rainbow: Some Early Cautionary Lessons Learned.' This seems to go beyond FUBAR."

"It's governmentese for 'Revive this project and watch your career die.' We won't be teleporting battleships again any time soon."

"Well, that explains Bob's mood." Sprague stroked his mustache, ignoring the younger man's puzzled look. "But, Isaac, don't you think that's a terrible shame? Imagine the adventures you're missing out on. I would have loved to have gone with you on your little jaunt."

"No, you wouldn't. Oh, there are worse things to look at than bare-breasted girl pirates, I'll grant you that. But when the god-creature first appeared, shrouded in darkness and rushing down upon us —"

"Made your blood run cold, eh?" Sprague began. But Asimov was shaking his head in an it's-not-that-way manner. "Well, humbling then, meeting a superior intellect like — no? Bob was ranting about how he wanted to go back with an arsenal."

"But that's it exactly! The first thing we did was to *shoot* at him! We didn't know he was hostile. But he was strange and different, and so we met him with violence. Can you imagine how much trouble the Navy could stir up with an entire fleet of teleporting battleships and the key to infinity?"

This was too much. "Isaac, you're a *science fiction writer!* How can you turn your back on all you've seen?"

"I'm afraid that for the good of humanity, our future journeys of exploration must henceforth take place solely in the realm of the imagination." Asimov spoke with the full gravitas of all his twenty-three years. Despite himself, Sprague, more than a decade older, couldn't help but smile. "The human race has to mature a little more before we can be allowed out into the larger universe. We have one World War to play with right now, and I think that's quite enough."

Before Sprague could think of an adequate response, Asimov looked at him with a troubled expression and blurted, "When did you grow a mustache?"

Astounded, Sprague said, "I had this mustache when we first met."

"I don't think so, Sprague. I always thought you might benefit from a little fur on the upper lip. Looks good."

"Isaac, you are the quintessence of the absent-minded professor! You get more forgetful by the hour." To change the subject from his friend's shortcomings, Sprague said, "So how did you spend Yom Kippur? Not at synagogue, presumably."

"I spent it at home, puttering around with the radio. Did you ever make a crystal radio set when you were young?"

"What boy didn't? A chunk of quartz, a safety pin, a rubber eraser and an earphone. Simplest thing in the world."

"Yes, and yet to look at the inside of a commercial radio, you'd think it was incredibly complicated. Well, I was thinking about the degaussing equipment, and it occurred to me that...." He made a final connection. "There!"

Green fire rippled over the radio, and it began to sink down through the surface of the desk.

Hastily, Asimov snatched it back up. He yanked a wire loose, and the device died.

Sprague's eyes felt like they were bulging out of their sockets. His mouth moved up and down, but no words came out.

Asimov raised a finger to his lips. "The Navy classified this top-secret, remember. We're not going to say another word on this matter."

And they never did. ⬦

I think I was set up, but I've never dared inquire too deeply.

Ellen Datlow needed round-robin stories for her *Event Horizon* website. "It'll be easy," Ellen said. "No advance planning. One person starts, and the next person takes off from there, then the next builds on the first two, and so on. Four people, three rounds each. We'll post the story to the website as you write it."

Michael Swanwick had a story idea that he'd always wanted to write. Susan Caspar, who had just finished a round-robin for Ellen, had an important piece of advice.

"Cheat," she said. "Plan it in advance. Work out the plot. Work out who'll write what. Don't make the same mistake we did."

"Ellen won't like that," I said.

"Lie," said Susan.

So we did.

Michael's idea galloped off from the fact that science-fiction greats Isaac Asimov and Robert Heinlein had actually been stationed at the Philadelphia Naval Base in 1943, the same year that the supposed "USS Eldridge" experiment took place.

We added Grace Hopper in the interest of gender balance: in reality, she joined the WAVES in December of 1943, a few months later than the story. She was one of the first computer engineers, the inventor of the compiler program, and, of course, is famous as the programmer who found the first actual bug in a computer (a moth), and taped it into the log-book.

We recruited Pat Murphy and Andy Duncan as the other two writers. Each of us would take a different point of view, to make any stylistic differences seem natural. I took Asimov, Andy took Heinlein, and Pat took Hopper. Michael would go last in each round, and toss in an unscripted hand-grenade of plot, just to keep us from getting complacent.

It was great fun. I had never known Asimov personally, but I talked to people who had, and read four volumes of his autobiographical writing. I got to like him quite a bit. He hated to travel – planes, trains, or automobiles – and it amused me no end to send him, brave as only the truly terrified can be, across the Sargasso Sea on the back of a giant sea turtle.

My thanks to Michael Swanwick, Pat Murphy, and Andy Duncan for permission to reprint the story here, and to Michael for providing the above-mentioned turtle.

Afterwards

Howard Waldrop

You don't know what a joy it is to write about Eileen Gunn.

For one thing, she's about the *only* writer I know who turns out stories even more slowly than I do, which is a rare thing in this damn field...

You've just read one long-overdue swell collection of her stuff: she's waited thirty-something years for it, and so have *you*.

As Bill told you in his foreword, and the quite-capable Ms. Gunn has explained in the story-notes themselves, these stories are the product of a vast number of synchronicities, coincidences, and of having one of the screwiest of odd-job histories in the Western world. (Eileen has oiled cucumbers in the Pike Place Market: lots of people have had *that* Seattle entry-level job: how many people you know who've done *that* also worked with Bill Gates when he was *still* in the garage, too?)

Peripatetic ain't the word for this gal (Cosmas Indicopluestes had nothing on her). When I first met her, she was living in Lompoc (or somewhere like that) in CA; then the letters were coming from Eugene OR; suddinkly (as Popeye would say) the return address was Seattle (where, haring off around the world all the time, she stayed for a couple of decades). In the last six years, suddinkly it's Brooklyn; a couple of clicks on the year-o-meter it's San Francisco; two more and she's back where she started in Rain City, where maybe she'll stay another decade or three...

She once took the Trans-Siberian Express, east-to-west (she speaks Russian at least as well as the average Kazakhstani). When she later went to Italy (she speaks Italian and Latin at least as well as the average Fescinni) the local commies threw her a block party because she'd actually been to Mother Russia...

All this to a lady who was born in Worcester (pronounced Were-chest-or) MA...

She knows *everything* about computers (and has for thirty years) without once being a dweeb about it, and I don't hold her computer-literacy against her. ("Computers and cell phones are, by and large," I said ten years ago, "there to make morons feel important.") She's designed some great web sites (I hear) and she's the editor/publisher of InfiniteMatrix.net, which you ought to check out.

This lady went to the Clarion SF Writers Workshop in the mid-'70s, and started selling stories as fast as she could write them after that (two, sometimes *three* a decade...). She's done penance ever since by being one of the directors of the Clarion West workshop on-and-off the last twenty years; a thankless damn job.

She's working on a biography of Avram Davidson, one of those truly great and irritable iconoclasts who occasionally grace this benighted field. She got to know him in the last few years of his life when their peripatets crossed and he lived a ferry-boat ride away in Bremerton. The book will be a wow.

Eileen's also, like me, been threatening people with novels for the last, say, 20–25 years now... (I've read parts of two of them and they're both swell: I want to read the whole things, *right now*.)

But the best of what she's done is in this here book you just read (you *are* reading this last, aren't you?). There's even the recipe from the Tiptree Bake Sale Book (and I know from personal experience she makes one mean cherry cobbler, too). There's "Nirvana High," which is a collaboration with Leslie What (who was at that same mid-'70s Clarion workshop and is just now publishing *her* first novel). There's also that rarity – a four-way collaboration that is *not* a joke-story, "Green Fire"; I don't know who did exactly what — I know that they made it work.

I either read, or heard Eileen read, an earlier version of "Computer Friendly" — I was doing my Sidney Greenstreet imitation for weeks afterwards ("I don't know what you're going to do, sir, but by gad, I'm sure it will be astounding, simply astounding! Meehehe-hee.") What I wasn't prepared for in this final version was the depth of feeling — nay, poignancy — of its central concept, and the seeming ease with which Ms. Gunn brought the whole thing off.

And she never ever takes the easy way out — there are plenty of mediocre writers out there who can do that, and fast, too! — she follows up on what the stories *want* to be saying.

Take "Fellow Americans," for instance. She wrote the story for the original anthology *Alternate Presidents*. (When it was published, the book had a wonderful, evocative cover of Thomas Dewey holding up the misprisioned *Chicago Tribune* with its headline, "Truman Defeats Dewey"...) On its surface, the story seems to be about Richard Nixon — *The Tricky Dick Show* — and there's Dan and Marilyn Quayle ("S. Danforth Quayle? Wasn't he the Mayor of Duckburg?" — Calvin Trillin) — and I guarantee, if you've read it, you'll *never* forget Nixon's story of taking LSD and Pat crying for the music trapped in the piano... But this is just the outside — fine as it is — of the story. Yeah, Dick Nixon was veep in the '50s, blew the '60 election, and the Senate try, entered showbiz. And Dan is the same dweeb veep he was when the story was written.

But the election Eileen chose to write about was the 1964 one. Goldwater won. Not only that; he was re-elected in '68. (It shows how much times have changed that, before his death a few years ago, the real Goldwater sounded like a *reasonable* man compared to the flaming Nazi gasbags who've taken over his Republican Party...) Eileen's story is Goldwater's story — the Party's story is Nixon's showbiz one. Goldwater was the Republicans' Harry S Truman, setting up, in Gore Vidal's word, The Imperial State — the one we've been living with the last 40 years or so.

This was the quietest (and funniest) story in an anthology not noted otherwise for subtlety. (As someone once said, in American politics, there are *still* people pissed off about the Compromise of 1850 and the Gadsden Purchase...) Ms. Gunn took a Cold Hard Look at the Whole Thing, not just the alternate election she wrote about. She did not do the Easy Thing — which would have been: Goldwater and Nuclear Defoliants in Viet Nam.

And there's never been a story like the title one of this collection. It's pure distillation of the '80s/'90s Power Cleavage/Dress for Success syndrome which swept the business schools and worlds like that year's Tortilla and Screen Door Jesuses. The story has something to *say*.

As do they all.

It's so good to finally have them all in one place you can reach for in the bookshelf, instead of looking in ten or twelve anthologies and magazines.

I couldn't be prouder of Eileen, or of this collection, if it were of me, and this book was one of mine. ⸙

March 30, 2004

EILEEN GUNN is a short-story writer and the editor/publisher of the cutting-edge website *The Infinite Matrix*, www.infinitematrix .net. "Stable Strategies for Middle Management" and "Computer Friendly," included in this collection, were nominated for the Hugo Award.

In the mid-1980s, she was Director of Advertising and Sales Promotion at Microsoft Corporation. Her stories often draw on her understanding of the Byzantine dynamics of the corporate workplace.

Since 1988, she has served on the board of directors of the internationally known Clarion West Writers Workshop. She is at work on a biography of the fantasist Avram Davidson.

Her personal website can be found at www.eileengunn.com.

"There is no sense trying to sum up Eileen Gunn: she's too damn various. She wrote *the* manual on corporate infighting, Kafka style. In these pages, she reveals the secret careers of Richard Nixon and Isaac Asimov, Barry Goldwater and Robert A. Heinlein. Gunn slipstreams effortlessly and was writing about post-humanity long before Vernor Vinge gave the singularity a name. What you have here is a chest that contains the many treasures of one of our most nimble writers. Open it and be dazzled!"

– JAMES PATRICK KELLY, author of *Think Like a Dinosaur!*

"Eileen Gunn, a perspicacious editor, has such good taste that she can't make herself write enough fiction. Encourage her by reading this right away."

– BRUCE STERLING, author of *The Zenith Angle*

"Eileen's stories: a diamond here, sparkling all the way through; a geode there, stony outside, sharp and brilliant within; and at a distance a piece of amber...with a scorpion inside, still ready and able to strike."

– VONDA N. MCINTYRE, author of *The Moon and the Sun*